I0599178

Edward Bulwer Lytton, Edwin Booth

Bulwer's Drama of Richelieu

Vol. 1

Edward Bulwer Lytton, Edwin Booth

Bulwer's Drama of Richelieu
Vol. 1

ISBN/EAN: 9783337334338

Printed in Europe, USA, Canada, Australia, Japan

Cover: Foto ©Andreas Hilbeck / pixelio.de

More available books at **www.hansebooks.com**

The Prompt-Book.

Edited by William Winter.

✠

Bulwer's Drama

of

Richelieu

As Presented by

Edwin Booth.

✠

" *I was born*
Beneath the aspect of a bright-eyed star,
And my triumphant adamant of soul
Is but the fixed persuasion of success."

" *Like the old fisher of the fable, Proteus,*
Netting great Neptune's wariest tribes, and
changing
Into all shapes when craft pursued himself."

" *He had a way with him — a something*
That always —"

" *There is a strife in which the loftiest look*
Is the most subtle armour."

" *The power which in the age of iron*
Burst forth, to curb the great and raise the low."

✠

New - York :
Printed, for William Winter, by
Francis Hart & Company, 63 and 65 Murray Street.
1878.

Preface.

*T*HE full title of this piece is "Richelieu; or, The Conspiracy." It was written in the fall of 1838, and it was first acted on March 7th, 1839. Macready—for whom, and under whose counsel it had been made—brought it out, at Covent Garden, London, of which theatre he was then the manager, and himself personated Richelieu. In Macready's "Reminiscences" there are several interesting allusions to this subject, notable as showing in what manner the drift of the play was changed by the author, under the actor's advice, and also as showing that the text was freely cut, in the process of adapting it to the practical uses of the stage. "When I developed the whole plan of alterations," says Macready, the author "was in ecstacy." This, evidently, was an instance in which the literary faculty was happily guided by an experienced and just dramatic instinct. In this drama, consequently, the story is told by direct action, out of which the language naturally flows,—tinged, it is true, with the romantic sentimentalism that thoroughly saturated Bulwer's thought and style,—and to which, for the most part, it is a spontaneous necessity. It appears to have been Macready's impression that Bulwer had drawn, under the name of Richelieu, a character entirely different from the historic original; but he records that

Bulwer at length satisfied him as to the justice of the portrayal, from the evidence of history. There is no doubt, however, that the poet has considerably—though neither unjustly nor inartistically—idealized the character of Richelieu. His own remarks upon it, in his essays upon "Self-Controul" and "Posthumous Reputation," in "Caxtoniana," illustrate this truth. "In Richelieu," he says, " there was no genuine self-controul; because he had made his whole self the puppet of certain fixed and tyrannical ideas." Yet the Richelieu of this play is iron in his domination of self and of circumstance. In the play, moreover, the cruelty of the Cardinal nowhere appears, while his craft and vanity are much softened. He is made, in fact, the ideal hero of a poetical work, and he should be regarded solely in this light. The text of the original has been cut and arranged in accordance with this idea, and with the plan of action pursued by Edwin Booth. This version differs from those · used by Macready and Forrest, and it also differs from all others in print or in use. The purpose which has governed in the editorial work was the purpose to give all possible prominence to the poetical aspect of the character. As to particular modifications: the long monologue that begins Act Third has been shortened to a few carefully chosen lines; several minor scenes and several clusters of superfluous lines have been omitted; and the characters of the Governor and Gaoler of the Bastile have been excised. The year of the play is indicated by the reference, in Act Fifth, to the loss, by Charles I., of " a battle that decides one-half his realm." The earliest of the Parliamentary victories that could with propriety be so designated was the battle of Marston Moor, fought on July 2d, 1644. Bulwer, it must be assumed, intended to take a poetic license with history, since, while no other battle than that is responsive to his allusion, both Richelieu and Louis XIII. were dead before that battle was fought, before any important battle had signalized the strife betwixt Charles I. and the Puritans, and before Cromwell had become known. Louis XIII., of France, reigned from 1610 to 1643. Richelieu died in 1642, aged 57. Cromwell, even at Marston Moor, was but second in command. Richelieu, it is probable, never heard of him. This drama was first acted in America, September 4th, 1839, at Wallack's National Theatre, in Leonard Street, New-York. Edwin Forrest was then the representative of the Cardinal.

> *" Vivet extento Proculeius aevo,*
> *Notus in frates animi paterni."*

W. W.

New-York, March 9th, 1878.

❖

"The purest treasure mortal times afford
Is spotless reputation : that away,
Men are but gilded loam or painted clay.
A jewel in a ten-times barred-up chest
Is a bold spirit in a loyal breast.
Mine honour is my life ; both grow in one :
Take honour from me and my life is done."—SHAKESPEARE.

"To him the church, the realm, their power consign ;
Through him the rays of regal bounty shine ;
Turned by his nod, the stream of honour flows :
His smile alone security bestows :
Still to new heights his restless wishes tower :
Claim leads to claim, and power advances power."

DR. JOHNSON.

"The brave man carves out his fortune, and every man is the son of his own works."—CERVANTES.

"A fiery soul, which, working out its way,
Fretted the pigmy body to decay,
And o'er-informed the tenement of clay."—DRYDEN.

"Conceal not Time's misdeeds, but on my brow
Retrace his mark ;
Let the retiring hair be silvery now,
That once was dark :
Eyes that reflected images too bright,
Let clouds o'ercast,
And from the tablet be abolished quite,
The cheerful past."—LANDOR.

"Old as I am, I know what passion is.
It is the summer's heat, sir, which in vain
We look for frost in."—SHERIDAN KNOWLES.

"Cardinal Richelieu's politics made France the terror of Europe."

ADDISON.

"He who ascends to mountain-tops shall find
The loftiest peaks most wrapped in clouds and snow ;
He who surpasses or subdues mankind
Must look down on the hate of those below.
Though high above the sun of glory glow,
And far beneath the earth and ocean spread,
Round him are icy rocks, and loudly blow
Contending tempests on his naked head,
And thus reward the toils which to those summits led."

LORD BYRON.

❖

Persons Represented.

✠

LOUIS XIII., KING OF FRANCE.

GASTON, DUKE OF ORLEANS, *brother to the King.*

CARDINAL RICHELIEU.

BARADAS, *the King's favourite.*

ADRIAN DE MAUPRAT, *an officer in the French Army.*

DE BERINGHEN, *a courtier.*

JOSEPH, *a Capuchin, confidant to Richelieu.*

HUGUET, *an officer and a spy in Richelieu's service.*

FRANÇOIS, *a Page to Richelieu.*

FIRST COURTIER.

FIRST CONSPIRATOR.

CAPTAIN OF THE GUARD.

FIRST, SECOND, AND THIRD SECRETARIES OF STATE.

JULIE DE MORTEMAR, *an orphan, ward to Richelieu.*

MARION DE LORME, *a spy for Richelieu.*

COURTIERS, PAGES, CONSPIRATORS, OFFICERS, SOLDIERS,
GENTLEMEN, AND ATTENDANTS.

Place and Time.

✠

SCENE.—*Paris and Ruelle* [*Reuil*], *in France.*

PERIOD.—*Middle of the Seventeenth Century.*

TIME OF ACTION.—*Four days.*

SCENES REQUIRED.—*First Act, two ; Second Act, two ;
Third Act, one ; Fourth Act, one ; Fifth Act, one. The
principal scene set for Act First is used again in Act
Second.*

RICHELIEU.

❖

Act First.

FIRST DAY.

Scene First. { Paris. A Room in the House of Marion De Lorme. Baradas and Orleans at table r. Marion De Lorme conversing with a Courtier c. De Beringhen, De Mauprat, and Courtiers playing at dice l. Courtiers looking on.

       Orl.   *[Drinking.*

Here's to our enterprize!

       Bar.   *[Glancing at Marion.*

Hush, sir!

       Orl.   *[Aside.*

Nay, count.
You may trust her; she doats on me; no house
So safe as Marion's.

       Bar.

Still, we have a secret;
And oil and water—woman and a secret—
Are hostile properties.

       Orl.

Well—Marion, see
How the play prospers yonder.

       [Marion goes to the table l.

Bar.   [*Producing a parchment.*

I have now
All the conditions drawn; it only needs
Our signatures.
Bouillon will join his army with the Spaniard,
March on to Paris: there, dethrone the king;
You will be regent; I, and ye, my lords
Form the new council.   So much for the core
Of our great scheme.

Orl.

But Richelieu is an Argus;
One of his hundred eyes will light upon us,
And then—good-by to life.

Bar.

To gain the prize
We must destroy the Argus :—ay, my lord,
The scroll the core, but blood must fill the veins
Of our design : while this dispatched to Bouillon,
Richelieu dispatched to Heaven !   The last *my* charge.
Meet here to-morrow night.   *You*, sir, as first
In honour and in hope, meanwhile select
Some trusty knave to bear the scroll to Bouillon :
'Midst Richelieu's foes, *I 'll* find some desperate hand
To strike for vengeance, while we stride to power.

Orl.

So be it :—to-morrow, midnight.—Come, my lords.
        [*Exeunt Orleans, and the courtiers in his train.
        Those at the other table rise, salute Orleans, as
        he passes out, and reseat themselves.   Baradas
        goes to table* L, *and watches the game.*

De Ber.

Double the stakes.

De Maup.

Done.

De Ber.

Bravo ; faith, it shames me
To bleed a purse already *in extremis.*

De Maup.

Nay, as you 've had the patient to yourself
So long, no other doctor should dispatch it.

[*De Mauprat throws and loses.*

Omnes.

Lost !   Ha, ha — poor De Mauprat !

De Ber.

One throw more ?

De Maup.

No ; I am bankrupt:
There goes all except   [*Pushing gold.*
My honour and my sword.

De Ber.

Ay, take the sword
To Cardinal Richelieu : — he gives gold for steel,
When worn by brave men.

De Maup.

[*Rises and goes to table* R.

Richelieu !

De Ber.   [*To Baradas.*

At that name
He changes colour, bites his nether lip.
Ev'n in his brightest moments whisper " Richelieu,"
And you cloud all his sunshine.

Bar.

I have marked it,
And I will learn the wherefore.

De Maup.

The Egyptian
Dissolved her richest jewel in a draught :[1]
Would I could so melt time and all its treasures,
And drain it thus.   [*Drinking.*

De Ber.

Come, gentlemen, what say ye ;
A walk on the Parade ?

Omnes.

Ay, come, De Mauprat.

De Maup.

Pardon me; we shall meet again, ere night-fall.

Bar.

I 'll stay and comfort Mauprat.

De Ber.

Comfort ! — When
We gallant fellows have run out a friend,
There 's nothing left — except to run him through !
There 's the last act of friendship.

De Maup.

Let me keep
That favour in reserve; in all beside
Your most obedient servant.

[*Exeunt all but De Mauprat and Baradas.*

[N. B.—*The scene is sometimes changed, at this
point, to facilitate the setting of the room in
Richelieu's palace.*]

Bar.

You have lost—
Yet are not sad.

De Maup.

Sad! —Life and gold have wings,
And must fly one day ; — open then, their cages,
And wish them merry.

Bar.

You 're a strange enigma ;
Fiery in war and yet to glory lukewarm ;
All mirth in action ; in repose all gloom.

Fortune of late has severed us — and led
Me to the rank of courtier, count, and favourite,
You to the titles of the wildest gallant
And bravest knight in Fránce: are you content?
No; — trust in me — some gloomy secret——

De Maup.

Ay; —
A secret that doth haunt me, as of old,
Men were possessed of fiends: where'er I turn,
The grave yawns dark before me. — I *will* trust you:
Hating the Cardinal, and beguiled by Orleans,
You know I joined the Languedoc revolt —
Was captured — sent to the Bastile——

Bar.

But shared
The general pardon, which the Duke of Orleans
Won for himself, and all in the revolt
Who but obeyed his orders.

De Maup.

Note the phrase:
"*Obeyed his orders.*"   Well, when on my way
To join the duke in Languedoc, I (then
The down upon my lip — less man than boy),
Leading young valours, reckless as myself,
Seized on the town of Faviaux, and displaced
The royal banners for the rebel.   Orleans,
Never too daring, when I reached the camp,
Blamed me for acting — mark — *without his orders.*
Upon this quibble, Richelieu razed my name
Out of the general pardon.

Bar.

Yet released you
From the Bastile——

2

De Maup.

To call me to his presence
And thus address me : — "You have seized a town
Of France, without the orders of your leader ;
And for this treason, but one sentence — Death."

Bar.

Death !

De Maup.

" I have pity on your youth and birth,
Nor wish to glut the headsman : join your troop,
Now on the march against the Spaniards ; change
The traitor's scaffold for the soldier's grave :
Your memory stainless — they who shared your crime
Exiled or dead — your king shall never learn it."

Bar.

O tender pity — O most charming prospect !
Blown into atoms by a bomb, or drilled
Into a cullendar by gunshot ! — Well ?

De Maup.

You have heard if I fought bravely.   Death became
Desired, as Daphne by the eager Daygod.[2]
Like him I chased the nymph — to grasp the laurel !
I could not die !

Bar.

Poor fellow !

De Maup.

When the Cardinal
Reviewed the troops, his eyes met mine ; he frowned,
Summoned me forth: " How 's this ? " quoth he : " you
      have shunned
The sword — beware the axe ! 't will fall one day !"
He left me thus; we were recalled to Paris,
And — you know all !

Bar.

And, knowing this, why halt you,
Spelled by the rattlesnake, while in the breasts
Of your firm friends beat hearts that vow the death
Of your grim tyrant ?—wake : be one of us ;
The time invites : the king detests the Cardinal,
Dares not disgrace, but groans to be delivered
Of that too great a subject : join your friends,
Free France, and save yourself.

De Maup.

Hush ! Richelieu bears
A charmèd life : to all who have braved his power
One common end — the block !

Bar.

Nay, if he live,
The block your doom.

De Maup.

Better the victim, count,
Than the assassin : France requires a Richelieu,
But does not need a Mauprat. Truce to this :
All time one midnight, where my thoughts are spectres :
What to me fame ?—what love ?—

Bar.

Yet dost thou not love?

De Maup.

Love ?—I am young——

Bar.

And Julie fair ! [*Aside.*] It is so.
Upon the margin of the grave, his hand
Would pluck the rose that *I* would win and wear ! [*Aloud.*
Thou lovest ——

De Maup. [*Gaily.*

No more !
I love : Your breast holds both my secrets : never
Unbury either ! — Come, while yet we may,

We 'll bask us in the noon of rosy life ;
Lounge through the gardens, flaunt in the taverns,
Laugh, game, drink, feast : if so confined my days,
Faith, I 'll enclose the nights.   Pshaw, not so grave ;
I 'm a true Frenchman !—*Vive la bagatelle !*
                    [*Enter Huguet and guards* L.

Hug.

Messire De Mauprat,—I arrest you !— Follow
To the lord Cardinal.

De Maup.

You see, my friend,
I 'm out of my suspense ; the tiger 's played
Long enough with his prey.   Farewell !   Hereafter
Say, when men name me, " Adrian De Mauprat
Lived without hope, and perished without fear !"
            [*Exeunt De Mauprat, Huguet, and guards,* L.

Bar.

Farewell !   I trust forever !   I designed thee
For Richelieu's murderer — but as well his martyr !
In childhood you the stronger, and I cursed you ;
In youth the fairer, and I cursed you still ;
And now my rival : while the name of Julie
Hung on thy lips, I smiled — for then I saw,
In my mind's eye, the cold and grinning Death,
Hang o'er thy head the pall !   Ambition, love,
Ye twin-born stars of daring destinies,
Sit in my house of life !   By the king's aid
I will be Julie's husband, in despite
Of my lord Cardinal.   By the king's aid
I will be minister of France, in spite
Of my lord Cardinal ; and then ; what then ?
The king loves Julie ; feeble prince ! false master !
Then, by the aid of Bouillon, and the Spaniard,
I will dethrone the king ; and all — ha ! — ha !
All, in despite of my lord Cardinal.
                        [*Scene changes.*

Scene Second. { PARIS. A ROOM IN THE PALACE OF CARDINAL RICHELIEU.

[*Enter Richelieu and Joseph.*

Rich.

And so you think this new conspiracy
The craftiest trap yet laid for the old fox?
Fox! well, I like the nickname: what did Plutarch
Say of the Greek Lysander?

Jos.

I forget.

Rich.

That where the lion's skin fell short, he eked it
Out with the fox's! A great statesman, Joseph,
That same Lysander.

Jos.

Orleans heads the traitors.

Rich.

A very wooden head, then! Well?

Jos.

The favourite,
Count Baradas—

Rich.

A weed of hasty growth.
First gentleman of the chamber,—titles, lands,
And the king's ear. It cost me six long winters
To mount as high as in six little moons [4]
This painted lizard: but I hold the ladder,
And when I shake he falls: what more?

Jos.

A scheme
To make your orphan-ward an instrument
To aid your foes.
Your ward has charmed the king.

Rich.

Out on you!
Have I not, one by one, from such fair shoots,
Plucked the insidious ivy of his love?
And shall it creep around my blossoming tree,
Where innocent thoughts, like happy birds, make music
That spirits in heaven might hear?
The king is weak: whoever the king loves
Must rule the king; the lady loves another;
The other rules the lady: thus we 're balked
Of our own proper sway.   The king must have
No goddess but the state:—the state! that 's Richelieu![5]

Jos.

This is not the worst: Louis, in all decorous,
And deeming you her least compliant guardian,
Would veil his suit by marriage with his minion,
Your prosperous foe, Count Baradas!

Rich.

Ha! ha!
I have another bride for Baradas!

Jos.

You, my lord?

Rich.

Ay—more faithful than the love
Of fickle woman; when the head lies lowest,
Clasping him fondest: sorrow never knew
So sure a soother; and her bed is stainless!

[*Enter François* C.

Fran.

Mademoiselle De Mortemar!

Rich.

Most opportune: admit her.   [*Exit François* C.
In my closet
You 'll find a rosary, Joseph; ere you tell

Three hundred beads, I 'll summon you.   Stay, Joseph;
I did omit an Ave in my matins,—
A grievous fault; atone it for me, Joseph;
There is a scourge within; I am weak, you strong;
It were but charity to take my sin
On such broad shoulders.

Jos.

I ! guilty of such criminal presumption
As to mistake myself for you!   No, never !
Think it not !   [*Aside.*]   Troth, a pleasant invitation !
[*Exit Joseph* L.   *Enter Julie De Mortemar* C.

Rich.

That 's my sweet Julie !

Julie.

Are you gracious ?   [*Placing herself at his feet.*
May I say " Father ? "

Rich.

Now and ever !

Julie.

Father !
A sweet word to an orphan.

Rich.

No, not orphan
While Richelieu lives : thy father loved me well ;
My friend, ere I had flatterers : now I 'm great,
In other phrase, I 'm friendless : he died young
In years, not service, and bequeathed thee to me ;
And thou shalt have a dowry, girl, to buy
Thy mate amid the mightiest.   Drooping ?—sighs ?—
Art thou not happy at the court ?

Julie.

Not often.

Rich.   [*Aside.*

Can she love Baradas?   Ah! at thy heart   [*To Julie.*
There's what can smile and sigh, blush and grow pale,
All in a breath.   Thou art admired—art young.
Does not his majesty commend thy beauty;
Ask thee to sing to him?

Julie.

He's very tiresome,
Our worthy king.

Rich.

Fie!   Kings are never tiresome
Save to their ministers.   What courtly gallants
Charm ladies most?   De Sourdiac, Longueville, or
The favourite, Baradas?

Julie.

A smileless man—I
Fear and shun him.

Rich.

Yet he courts thee!

Julie.

Then—
He is more tiresome than his majesty.

Rich.

Right, girl; shun Baradas.   Yet of these flowers
Of France, not one, in whose more honeyed breath
Thy heart hears summer whisper?

             [*Enter Huguet* C.

Hug.

The Chevalier De Mauprat waits below.

Julie.   [*Starting up, in alarm.*

De Mauprat!

Rich.

Hem !
He has been tiresome too !   Anon.

[Exit Huguet c.

Julie.

What doth he ?
I mean — I — does your eminence — that is —
Know you Messire de Mauprat ?

Rich.

Well ! — and you —
Has he addressed you often ?

Julie.

Often !   No —
Nine times : nay, ten ; the last time by the lattice
Of the great staircase.   *[In a melancholy tone.*
The court sees him rarely.

Rich.

A bold and forward roister !

Julie.

He ? nay, modest,
Gentle and sad, methinks.

Rich.

Wears gold and azure ?

Julie.

No, sable.

Rich.

So, you note his colours, Julie ?
Shame on you, child, look loftier.   By the mass,
I have business with this modest gentleman.

Julie.

You 're angry with poor Julie : there 's no cause.

Rich.

No cause ! you hate my foes ?

3

Julie.

I do.

Rich.

Hate Mauprat.

Julie.

Not Mauprat: no, not Adrian, father.

Rich.

Adrian?   [*Julie moves toward* C.
Familiar!   Go, child; no,—not *that* way; wait
In the tapestry chamber: I will join you,—go.

Julie.   [*Going* R.

His brows are knit; I dare not call him father.
But I *must* speak.   Your eminence—

Rich.   [*Sternly.*

Well, girl!

Julie.

Nay,
Smile on me—one smile; there, now I'm happy.
Do not rank Mauprat with your foes; he is not;
I know he *is* not; he loves France too well.

Rich.

Not rank De Mauprat with my foes?
So be it.
I'll blot him from that list.

Julie.

That's my own father.
                     [*Exit Julie* R. I. E.

Rich.   [*Ringing bell on table.*

Huguet!
                     [*Enter Huguet* C.
De Mauprat struggled not, nor murmured?

Hug.

No: proud and passive.

Rich.

Bid him enter.   Hold:
Look that he hide no weapon.   Humph; despair
Makes victims sometimes victors.   When he has entered,
Glide round unseen; place thyself yonder; watch him;

[Pointing R.

If he show violence — (let me see thy carbine:

[Takes, examines, and returns Huguet's carbine.

So; a good weapon); if he play the lion,
Why — the dog's death.

[Exit Huguet C. *Richelieu slowly arranges papers
before him.   Enter De Mauprat* C., *preceded
by Huguet, who then retires* R. *and conceals
himself.*

Rich.

Approach, sir.   Can you call to mind the hour,
Now three years since, when in this room, methinks,
Your presence honoured me?

De Maup.

It is, my lord,
One of my most ——

Rich.   *[Dryly.*

Delightful recollections.[6]

De Maup.   *[Aside.*

St. Denis! doth he make a jest of axe and headsman?

Rich.   *[Sternly.*

I did then accord you
A mercy ill requited.
Messire de Mauprat,
Doomed to sure death, how have you since consumed
The time allotted you for serious thought
And solemn penance?

De Maup.   *[Embarrassed.*

The time, my lord?

Rich.

Is not the question plain ?   I 'll answer for thee.
Thou hast sought nor priest nor shrine ; no sackcloth
    chafed
Thy delicate flesh : the rosary and the death's head
Have not, with pious meditation, purged
Earth from the carnal gaze.   What thou hast *not* done
Brief told ; what done, a volume !   Wild debauch,
Turbulent riot : for the morn the dice-box ;
Noon claimed the duel, and the night the wassail :
These your most holy, pure preparatives
For death and judgment.   Do I wrong you, sir ?

De Maup.

I was not always thus : if changed my nature,
Blame that which changed my fate.   Alas, my lord,
Were you accursed with that which you inflicted —
By bed and board dogged by one ghastly spectre,
The while within you youth beat high, and life
Grew lovelier from the neighbouring frown of death —
The heart no bud, nor fruit, save in those seeds
Most worthless, which spring up, bloom, bear, and wither
In the same hour — were this your fate, perchance,
You would have erred, like me !

Rich.

I might, like you,
Have been a brawler and a reveller ; not,
Like you, a trickster and a thief.

De Maup. [*Advancing, threateningly.*

Lord Cardinal,
Unsay those words !
                    [*Huguet emerges and raises his carbine.*

Rich.   [*Raises his hand.*

Not quite so quick, friend Huguet ;
Messire de Mauprat is a patient man,
And he can wait.
You have outrun your fortune :   [*To De Mauprat.*

I blame you not that you would be a beggar—
Each to his taste; but I do charge you, sir,
That, being beggared, you would coin false moneys
Out of that crucible, called debt: to live
On means not yours; be brave in silks and laces,
Gallant in steeds, splendid in banquets;—all
Not yours; ungiven, uninherited, unpaid for:
This is to be a trickster; and to filch
Men's art and labour, which to them is wealth,
Life, daily bread,—quitting all scores with—" Friend,
You 're troublesome!" Why this, forgive me,
Is what—when done with a less dainty grace—
Plain folks call " *Theft!*" You owe ten thousand pis-
    toles,
Minus one crown, two liards!

De Maup.   [*Aside.*

The old conjurer!

Rich.

This is scandalous,
Shaming your birth and blood. I tell you, sir,
That you must pay your debts.

De Maup.

With all my heart,
My lord: where shall I borrow, then, the money ?

Rich.   [*Aside, and smiling.*

A humourous dare-devil: the very man
To suit my purpose; ready, frank, and bold.

[*To De Mauprat, and rising.*

Adrian de Mauprat, men have called me cruel;
I am not; I am just. I found France rent asunder;
The rich men despots and the poor banditti;
Sloth in the mart and schism within the temple;
Brawls festering to rebellion; and weak laws
Rotting away with rust in antique sheaths.
I have re-created France; and from the ashes
Of the old feudal and decrepit carcass,
Civilization on her luminous wings

Soars, phœnix-like, to Jove! What was my art?
Genius, some say; some, fortune; 'witchcraft, some:
Not so; my art was justice! Force and fraud
Mis-name it cruelty: you shall confute them!
My champion you! You met me as your foe.
Depart my friend. You shall not die: France needs
    you.
You shall wipe off all stains; be rich, be honoured;
Be great: I ask, sir, in return, this hand,
                    [*De Mauprat kneels.*
To gift it with a bride, whose dower shall match,
Yet not exceed her beauty.

De Maup.   [*Hesitating.*

I, my lord —
I have no wish to marry.

Rich.

Surely, sir,
To die were worse.

De Maup.   [*Rises.*

Scarcely; the poorest coward
Must die; but knowingly to march to marriage —
My lord, it asks the courage of a lion!

Rich.

Traitor, thou triflest with me. I know all.
Thou hast dared to love my ward — my charge.

De Maup.

As rivers
May love the sunlight — basking in the beams,
And hurrying on.

Rich.

Thou hast told her of thy love?

De Maup.

My lord, if I had dared to love a maid,
Lowliest in France, I would not so have wronged her,
As bid her link rich life and virgin hope
With one, the deathman's gripe might, from her side,
Pluck at the nuptial altar.

Rich.

I believe thee :
Yet, since she knows not of thy love, renounce her ;
Take life and fortune with another.— Silent ?

De Maup.

Your fate has been one triumph : you know not
How blessed a thing it was in my dark hour
To nurse the one sweet thought you bid me banish.
Love hath no need of words ; nor less within
That holiest temple, the heaven-builded soul,
Breathes the recorded vow. Base knight, false lover
Were he who bartered all that brightened grief
Or sanctified despair, for life and gold.
Revoke your mercy ; I prefer the fate
I looked for.

     Rich.   *[To Huguet, sternly.*

Huguet, to the tapestry chamber
Conduct your prisoner.

         [To De Mauprat.

You will there behold
The executioner :— your doom be private —

         [Crosses to R.

And heaven have mercy on you !

     De Maup.

When I 'm dead,
Tell her I loved her —

     Rich.   *[Hiding his face.*

Keep such follies, sir,
•For fitter ears. Go.

De Maup.

Does he mock me?

[*Exeunt De Mauprat and Huguet* R. I. E.
[*Richelieu laughs.*

Rich.

Joseph,
Come forth.

[*Enter Joseph* L. I. E.

Methinks your cheek has lost its rubies, Joseph.
I fear you have been too lavish of the flesh;
The scourge is heavy.

Jos.

Pray you, change the subject.

Rich.

You good men are so modest! Well, to business.
Go instantly — deeds — notaries! — bid my stewards
Prepare my house by the Luzembourg — *my* house
No more! — a bridal present to my ward,
Who weds to-morrow.

Jos.

Weds? with whom?

Rich.

De Mauprat.

Jos.

A penniless husband.

Rich.

Bah! the mate for beauty
Should be a man and not a money-chest!
When her brave sire lay on his bed of death,
I vowed to be a father to his Julie;
And so he died — the smile upon his lips:
And when I spared the life of her young lover,
Methought I saw that smile again. Who else,
Look you, in all the court, who else so well,

Brave, or supplant the favourite; balk the king,
Baffle their schemes?   I have tried him: he has honour
   and courage.
Besides, he has taste, this Mauprat: when my play
Was acted — to dull tiers of lifeless gapers,
Who had no soul for poetry — I saw *him*
Applaud, in the proper places: trust me, Joseph,
He is a man of most uncommon promise!

Jos.

And yet your foe.

Rich.

Have I not foes enow?
Great men gain doubly when they make foes friends.
Remember my grand maxims: first employ
All methods to conciliate.[8]

Jos.

Failing these?

Rich.   [*Fiercely.*

All means to crush! as with the opening and
The clenching of this little hand I will
Crush the small venom of these stinging courtiers. —
So, so, we 've baffled Baradas.

Jos.

And when
Check the conspiracy?

Rich.

Check? check?   Full way to it.
Let it bud, ripen, flaunt i' the day, and burst
To fruit — the Dead Sea's fruit of ashes; ashes
Which I will scatter to the winds.
Go, Joseph;
When you return I have a feast for you;
The last great act of my great play: the verses,
Methinks, are fine.
Come, you shall hear the verses now.   [*Seating himself* L.

4

Jos.   [*Aside.*

Worse than the scourge!
Strange that so great a statesman
Should be so bad a poet.

Rich.

What dost thou say?

Jos.

That it is strange so great a statesman should
Be so sublime a poet.[9]

Rich.

O you rogue, you rogue!
But come, the verses now.

Jos.

My lord,
The deeds, the notaries.

Rich.

True, I pity you!
But business first, then pleasure.   [*Exit Joseph* C.

Rich.   [*Reading.*

Ah, sublime!
       [*Enter De Mauprat and Julie* R. I. E.

De Maup.

O, speak, my lord!   I dare not think you mock me.
And yet——   [*They kneel before him.*
       Rich.

This line must be considered.

Julie.

Are we not both your children?

Rich.

O, sir—you live!
       [*Affecting now to see them for the first time.*

De Maup.

Why, no ; methinks
Elysium is not life.

Julie.

He smiles ! you smile,
My father : from my heart forever, now,
I 'll blot the name of orphan.

Rich.

Rise, my children —
For ye are mine, mine both ; and in your sweet
And young delight, your love (life's first-born glory)
My own lost youth breathes musical.

De Maup.

I 'll seek
Temple and priest henceforward : were it but
To learn Heaven's choicest blessings.

Rich.

Thou shalt seek
Temple and priest right soon : the morrow's sun
Shall see across these barren thresholds pass
The fairest bride in Paris.   Go, my children :
Even *I* loved once : [10] be lovers while ye may.

[*To De Mauprat.*

How is it with you, sir ?   You bear it bravely :
You know it asks the courage of a lion.

[*Exeunt De Mauprat and Julie* C.

O, God-like power ! woe, rapture, penury, wealth,
Marriage, and death, for one infirm old man
Through a great empire to dispense — withhold —
As the will whispers !   And shall things, like motes
That live in my daylight ; lackeys of court wages ;
Dwarfed starvelings ; manikins, upon whose shoulders
The burden of a province were a load,
More heavy than the globe on Atlas, cast
Lots for my robes and sceptre ? — France, I love thee !
All earth shall never pluck thee from my heart !
My mistress, France ; my wedded wife, sweet France ;
Who shall proclaim divorce for thee and me !

CURTAIN.

Act Second.

Scene First. { PARIS. AN APARTMENT IN DE MAUP-
RAT'S HOUSE.

[*Enter Baradas* L.

Bar.

Mauprat's new home: too splendid for a soldier!
But o'er his floors, the while I stalk, methinks
My shadow spreads gigantic to the gloom
The old, rude towers of the Bastile cast far
Along the smoothness of the jocund day.
Well, thou hast 'scaped the fierce caprice of Richelieu!
But art thou further from the headsman, fool?
Thy secret I have whispered to the king:
Thy marriage makes the king thy foe: thou stand'st
On the abyss—and in the pool below
I see a ghastly, headless phantom mirrored,—
Thy likeness, ere the marriage moon hath waned.
Meanwhile—meanwhile—ha, ha! if thou art wedded,
Thou art not wived!

[*Enter De Mauprat* R.

De Maup.

Was ever fate like mine?—
So blessed, and yet so wretched!

Bar.

Joy, De Mauprat!
Why, what a brow, man, for your wedding-day!

De Maup.

Jest not.   Distraction!

Bar.

What! your wife a shrew
Already?   Courage, man—the common lot.

De Maup.

O, that she were less lovely, or less loved!

Bar.

Riddles again!

De Maup.

You know what chanced between
The Cardinal and myself. ·

Bar.

This morning brought
Your letter: faith, a strange account.   I laughed
And wept at once for gladness.

De Maup.

We were wed
At noon : the rite performed, came hither—scarce
Arrived, when——

Bar.

Well?——

De Maup.

Wide flew the doors, and lo!
Messire de Beringhen, and this epistle.

Bar.

'Tis the king's hand; the royal seal.

De Maup.

Read—read!

Bar.   [*Reading.*

"Whereas Adrian de Mauprat, colonel and chevalier
in our armies, being already guilty of high treason, by the
seizure of our town of Faviaux, has presumed, without our
knowledge, consent, or sanction, to connect himself by

marriage with Julie de Mortemar, a wealthy orphan, attached to the person of Her Majesty; we do hereby proclaim and declare the said marriage contrary to law. On penalty of death, Adrian de Mauprat will not communicate with the said Julie de Mortemar by word or letter, save in the presence of our faithful servant, the Sieur de Beringhen, and then with such respect and decorum as are due to a demoiselle attached to the Court of France: until such time as it may suit our royal pleasure to confer with the Holy Church on the formal annulment of the marriage, and with our Council on the punishment to be awarded to Messire de Mauprat, who is cautioned, for his own sake, to preserve silence as to our injunction, more especially to Mademoiselle de Mortemar. Given under our hand and seal, at the Louvre.

"LOUIS."

[Gives back letter to De Mauprat.
Amazement! Did not Richelieu say the king
Knew not your crime?

De Maup.

He said so.

Bar.

Poor de Mauprat!
See you the snare, the vengeance worse than death
Of which you are the victim?

De Maup.

Ha!
Snare? vengeance,
Worse than death? Be plainer.

Bar.

What so clear?
Richelieu has but two passions.

De Maup.

Richelieu!

Bar. •

Yes.
Ambition and revenge: in you both blended.
First for ambition: Julie is his ward;
Innocent, docile, pliant to his will;
He placed her at the court; foresaw the rest:
The king loves Julie!

De Maup.

Merciful Heaven! The king!

Bar.

Such Cupids lend new plumes to Richelieu's wings:
But the court etiquette must give such Cupids
The veil of Hymen — Hymen but in name.
He looked abroad; found you his foe; thus served
Ambition — by the grandeur of his ward,
And vengeance — by dishonour to his foe.

De Maup.

Prove this.

Bar.

You have the proof — the royal letter;
Your strange exemption from the general pardon,
Known but to me and Richelieu: can you doubt
Your friend, to acquit your foe? .The truth is glaring:
Richelieu alone could tell the princely lover
The tale which sells your life, — or buys your honour.

De Maup.

I see it all: mock pardon — hurried nuptials —
False bounty! — all! — the serpent of that smile:
O! it stings home!

Bar.

You shall crush his malice:
Our plans are sure; Orleans is at our head;
We meet to-night; join us and with us triumph.

De Maup.

To-night!—O heaven!—my marriage night!—Revenge.
But the king? but Julie?

Bar.

The king? infirm in health, in mind more feeble,
Is but the plaything of a minister's will.
Were Richelieu dead, his power were mine; and Louis
Soon should forget his passion and your crime.
But whither now?

De Maup.

I know not; I scarce hear thee;
A little while for thought: anon I'll join thee;
But now, all air seems tainted, and I loathe
The face of man!

          [*Exit De Mauprat* L.

Bar.

Start from the chase, my prey!
But as thou speed'st, the hell-hounds of revenge
Pant in thy track and drag thee down.

          [*Enter De Beringhen* R.

De Ber.

Chevalier,
Your cook's a miracle: what, my host gone?
Faith, count, my office is a post of danger:
A fiery fellow, Mauprat! touch and go,—
Match and saltpeter,—pr-r-r-r!

Bar.

You
Will be released ere long. The king resolves
To call the bride to court this day.

De Ber.

Poor Mauprat!
Yet, since you love the lady, why so careless
Of the king's suit?

Bar.

Because the lady's virtuous,
And the king timid : ere he win the suit
He 'll lose the crown; the bride will be a widow;
And I — the Richelieu of the Regent Orleans.

De Ber.

Is Louis still so chafed against the fox,
For snatching yon fair dainty from the lion?

Bar.

So chafed that Richelieu totters. Yes, the king,
Is half conspiring against the Cardinal.
Enough of this. I 've found the man we wanted;
The man to head the hands that murder Richelieu ;
The man whose name's the synonym for daring.

De Ber.   [*Alarmed.*

He must mean me! No, count, I am, I own,
A valiant dog — but still —

Bar.

Whom can I mean
But Mauprat? Mark, to-night we meet at Marion's ;
There shall we sign: thence send this scroll
To Bouillon.   [*Showing a paper.*
You 're in that secret — one of our new council.

De Ber.

But to admit the Spaniard, France's foe,
Into the heart of France — dethrone the king —
It looks like treason, and I smell the headsman.

Bar.

O, sir, too late to falter : when we meet
We must arrange the separate, coarser scheme,
For Richelieu's death. Of this dispatch De Mauprat
Must nothing learn. He only bites at vengeance,
And he would start from treason. We must post him
Without the door at Marion's — as a sentry ;
So, when his head is on the block, his tongue
Cannot betray our more august designs.

5

De Ber.

I 'll meet you, if the king can spare me. [*Aside.*] No!
I am too old a goose to play with foxes;
I 'll roost at home. Meanwhile, in the next room
There's a delicious pâté; let 's discuss it.

Bar.

Pshaw! a man filled with sublime ambition
Has no time to discuss your pâtés.

De Ber.

Pshaw.
And a man filled with a sublime pâté,
Has no time to discuss ambition.— Gad,
I have the best of it!

[*Exit De Beringhen* R.

Bar.

All is made clear; Mauprat *must* murder Richelieu —
Die for that crime : I shall console his Julie.
This will reach Bouillon!—from the wrecks of France
I shall carve out — who knows — perchance a throne!
All in despite of my lord Cardinal.

[*Enter De Mauprat* L.

De Maup.

Speak! can it be ? — Methought that from the terrace
I saw the carriage of the king — and Julie!
No! No! my frenzy peoples the void air
With its own phantom!

Bar.

Nay, too true.— Alas!
Was ever lightning swifter, or more blasting,
Than Richelieu's forkèd guile ?

De Maup.

I 'll to the Louvre——

Bar.

And lose all hope! The Louvre!— the sure gate
To the Bastile!

De Maup.

The king.

Bar.

Is but the wax,
Which Richelieu stamps : break the malignant seal,
And I will raze the print.   Come, man, take heart!
Her virtue well could brave a sterner trial
Than a few hours of cold, imperious courtship.
Were Richelieu dust — no danger!

De Maup. •

Ghastly vengeance!
To thee and thine august and solemn sister,
The unrelenting death, I dedicate
The blood of Armand Richelieu!   When dishonour
Reaches our hearths, law dies and murder takes
The angel shape of justice!

Bar.

Bravely said!
At midnight, Marion's! — Nay, I cannot leave thee
To thoughts that ——

De Maup.

Speak not to me! — I am yours!
But speak not!   There's a voice within my soul,
Whose cry could drown the thunder.   O, if men
Will play dark sorcery with the heart of man,
Let them, who raise the spell, beware the fiend!

[*Exeunt* L.   *Scene changes.*

Scene Second. { PARIS.   A ROOM IN THE PALACE OF CAR-
DINAL RICHELIEU.   THE SAME AS IN
ACT FIRST.   FRANÇOIS DISCOVERED
AT TABLE L. U. E.

[*Enter Richelieu and Joseph.*

Jos.

Yes ; — Huguet, taking his accustomed round,
Disguised as some plain burgher, heard these rufflers
Quoting your name : — he listened : " Pshaw," said one,

" We are to seize the Cardinal in his palace
To-morrow ! "—" How ? " the other asked ;—" You 'll
    hear
The whole design to-night : the Duke of Orleans
And Baradas have got the map of action
At their fingers' end."   " So be it," quoth the other,
" I will be there,—Marion de Lorme's—at midnight : "

Rich.

I have them, man, I have them !

Jos.

So they say
Of you, my lord :—believe me, that their plans
Are mightier than you deem : you must employ
Means no less vast to meet them !

Rich.

Bah ! in policy
We foil gigantic dangers, not by giants,
But dwarfs : the statues of our stately fortune
Are sculptured by the chisel —not the axe.[11]
Ah ! were I younger —by the knightly heart
That beats beneath these priestly robes,[12] I would
Have pastime with these cut-throats !   Yea, as when,
Lured to the ambush of the expecting foe,
I clove my pathway through the plumèd sea !
Reach me yon falchion, François —not that bauble
For carpet warriors — yonder —such a blade
As old Charles Martel might have wielded, when
He drove the Saracen from France.
      [*François brings to Richelieu a long two-handed
        sword.*
With this
I, at Rochelle, did hand to hand engage
The stalwart Englisher :[13] no mongrels, boy,
Those island mastiffs.   Mark the notch, a deep one,
His casque made here.   I shore him to the waist !

A toy — a feather, then !
          [*Tries to wield it, but sinks, overcome, into chair.*
You see, a child could
Slay Richelieu now.

                    Fran.

But now, at your command
Are other weapons, good my lord.

          Rich.   [*Lifting a pen.*
True, this !
Beneath the rule of men entirely great
The pen is mightier than the sword.   Behold
The arch enchanter's wand: itself a nothing;
But taking sorcery from the master hand —
To paralyze the Cæsars, and to strike
The loud earth breathless !   Take away the sword —
States can be saved without it !
          [*François takes the sword back to its place.   Clock
               strikes.*
' T is the hour —
Retire, sir.
          [*Exit François* L.   *A knock.   Joseph opens secret
               door.   Enter Marion de Lorme, through secret
               door.*
                    Jos.   [*Amazed.*

Marion de Lorme !
                    Rich.

Hist ! Joseph,
Keep guard.   [*Joseph closes door and retires* C.
My faithful Marion !

                    Marion.

Good, my lord,
They meet to night in my poor house: the Duke
Of Orleans heads them.

                    Rich.

Yes ; go on.

Marion.

His highness
Much questioned if I knew some brave, discreet,
And vigilant man, whose tongue could keep a secret,
And who had those twin qualities for service,
The love of gold, the hate of Richelieu.

Rich.

You ——

Marion.

Made answer, "Yes; my brother; bold and trusty;
Whose faith my faith could pledge:" the duke then
        bade me
Have him equipped and armed, well mounted, ready
This night to part for Italy.

Rich.

Ah! ——
Has Bouillon too turned traitor? — So methought.
What part of Italy?

Marion.

The Piedmont frontier,
Where Bouillon lies encamped.

Rich.   [*Aside.*

Now there is danger!
Great danger!   If he tamper with the Spaniard,
And Louis list not to my council, as,
Without sure proof he will not, France is lost!
What more?   [*To Marion.*

Marion.

Dark hints of some design to seize
Your person, in your palace: nothing clear:
His highness trembled while he spoke; the words
Did choke each other.

Rich.

So!   Who is the brother
You recommended to the duke?

Marion.

Whoever
Your eminence may father.

Rich.

Darling Marion! [14]
    [*Goes to the table, and returns with a purse.
      Marion affects to refuse, but presently accepts the
      purse.*
There—pshaw—a trifle! What an eye you have!
And what a smile!—Ah, you fair perdition—
'T is well I 'm old!

Marion.   [*Aside.*

What a great man he is!

Rich.

You are sure they meet?—the hour?

Marion.

At midnight.

Rich.

And
You will engage to give the duke's dispatch,
To whom I send?

Marion.

Ay, marry!

Rich.   [*Aside.*

Huguet? No:
He will be wanted elsewhere. Joseph?—zealous,
But too well known— too much the elder brother.
Mauprat?—alas! it is his wedding day.
François?— the man of men! unnoted, young:
Ambitious. [*Strikes bell.*] François!
         [*Enter François* L. I. E.

Rich.

Follow this fair lady.
Find him the suiting garments, Marion: take
My fleetest steed: arm thyself to the teeth:
A packet will be given you, with orders,
No matter what! The instant that your hand
Closes upon it, clutch it, like your honour,
Which death alone can steal, or ravish; set
Spurs to your steed — be breathless, till you stand
Again before me. Stay, sir, you will find me
Two short leagues hence, at Ruelle, in my castle.
Young man, be blithe! for — note me — from the hour
I grasp that packet, think your guardian star
Rains fortune on you!

Fran.

If I fail——

Rich.

Fail —
In the lexicon of youth, which fate reserves
For a bright manhood, there is no such word
As *fail!* — You will instruct him further, Marion.
Follow her — but at distance: speak not to her,
Till you are housed: farewell, boy! never say "*Fail*"
    again.

Fran.

I will not!

Rich.

That's my young hero!
          [*Exeunt François and Marion* R. U. E.
So, they would seize my person in this palace?
I cannot guess their scheme: — but my retinue
Is here too large: a single traitor could
          [*Strikes bell. Joseph enters* C.
Strike impotent the faith of thousands. — Joseph,
Art sure òf Huguet? — Think; we hanged his father.

Jos.

But you have bought the son; heaped favours on him.

Rich.

Trash!—favours past—that's nothing.   In his hours
Of confidence with you, has he named the favours
To come he counts on ?

Jos.

Yes—a colonel's rank,
And letters of nobility.

Rich.

What, Huguet ?
　　　[*Huguet enters* C, *but is unseen by the Cardinal
　　　and Joseph.*

Hug.

My own name: soft!　　　　　　　　[*Hides himself.*

Rich.

My bashful Huguet: that can never be !
We have him not the less: we 'll promise it —
And see the king withholds.   Yes,
We 'll count on Huguet.

Hug.　　　　　　　　　　　　[*Aside.*

To thy cost, deceiver.
　　　　　　　　　　　　　　[*Huguet retires.*

Rich.

You are right: this treason
Assumes a fearful aspect: but once crushed,
Its very ashes shall manure the soil
Of power, and ripen such full sheaves of greatness,
That all the summer of my fate shall seem
Fruitless, beside the autumn!

Jos.

The saints grant it!
　　　　　　　　　　　　　　[*Huguet advances.*

6

Hug.

My lord Cardinal,
Your eminence bade me seek you at this hour.

Rich.

Did I ?—True, Huguet.—So, you overheard
Strange talk amongst these gallants: snares and traps
For Richelieu ?—Well, we 'll balk them ; let me think ;—
The men at arms you head—how many ?

Hug.

Twenty, [15] my lord.

Rich.

All trusty ?

Hug.

Yes, for ordinary
Occasions: if for great ones, I would change
Three-fourths at least.

Rich.

Ay, what are great occasions ?

Hug.

Great bribes.

Rich.   [*To Joseph.*

Good lack, he knows some paragons
Superior to great bribes !

Hug.

True gentlemen,
Who have transgressed the laws, and value life,
And lack not gold ; your eminence alone
Can grant them pardon: *ergo*, you can trust them !

Rich.

Logic.   So be it—let this honest twenty
Be armed and mounted.
They do not strike till morning,

Yet I will shift the quarter: bid the grooms
Prepare the litter — I will hence to Ruelle
While daylight lasts: and one hour after midnight
You and your twenty saints shall seek me thither.
You 're made to rise! You are, sir; — eyes of lynx,
Ears of the stag, a footfall like the snow:
You are a valiant fellow; yea, a trusty,
Religious, exemplary, incorrupt,
And precious jewel of a fellow, Huguet!
If I live long enough, — ay, mark my words —
If I live long enough, you 'll be a colonel —

                [*Huguet bows very low.*

Noble, perhaps! — One hour, sir, after midnight.

Hug.

You leave me dumb with gratitude, my lord:
I 'll pick the trustiest [*aside*] Marion's house can furnish.

                [*Exit Huguet* c.

Rich.

Good: all favours,
If François be but bold, and Huguet honest.
Huguet I half suspect; he bowed too low;
'T is not his way.

Jos.

This is the curse, my lord
Of your high state; suspicion of all men.

Rich.   [*Sadly.*

True; true; my leeches bribed to poison, pages
To strangle me in sleep; my very king
(This brain the unresting loom, from which was woven
The purple of his greatness) leagued against me:
Old, childless, friendless, broken, all forsake —
All — all — but —

Jos.

What?

Rich.

The indomitable heart
Of Armand Richelieu!

Jos.

And Joseph——

Rich. [*After a pause.*

You —
Yes, I believe you — yes; for all men fear you,
And the world loves you not: and I, friend Joseph,
I am the only man, who could, my Joseph,
Make you a bishop. [16]   Come, we'll go to dinner,
And talk the while of methods to advance
Our mother church. [17]   Ah, Joseph — Bishop Joseph !
[*Exeunt* R. 1. E.

CURTAIN.

Act Third.

Scene First. { RUELLE. RICHELIEU'S CASTLE. A GOTHIC CHAMBER. MOONLIGHT SHINING THROUGH THE WINDOW. BED, ON DAIS C.

           Rich.   *[Reading.*

"In silence and at night the conscience feels
That life should soar to nobler ends than power."
So sayest thou, sage and sober moralist!   *[In soliloquy.*
But wert thou tried?
Ye safe and formal men,
Who write the deeds, and with unfeverish hand
Weigh in nice scales the motives of the great,
Ye cannot know what ye have never tried.
Alas, I am not happy: blanched and seared
Before my time; breathing an air of hate,
And seeing daggers in the eyes of men;
Bearding kings,
And braved by lackeys [18]; murder at my bed;
And lone amidst the mutitudinous web,
With the dread three — that are the fates who hold
The woof and shears — the monk, the spy, the headsman:
And this is power! Alas! I am not happy.
     [After a pause, during which he is convulsed with
        pain.
Ah! here! that spasm, again! How life and death
Do wrestle for me momently!
           [Turning again to his book.
Speak to me, moralist: I'll heed thy counsel.
Were it not best —
           [Enter François hastily L.

Philosophy, thou liest!   [*Flinging away the book.*
Quick — the dispatch! — Power! — Empire! Boy — the
    packet!

Fran.

Kill me, my lord!

Rich.

They knew thee — they suspected —
They gave it not——

Fran.

He gave it — *he* — the Count
De Baradas — with his own hand he gave it!

Rich.

Baradas!   Joy! out with it!

Fran.

Listen,
And then dismiss me to the headsman.

Rich.

Ha!
Go on.

Fran.

They led me to a chamber: there
Orleans and Baradas, and some half-score
Whom I knew not, were met——

Rich.

Not more!

Fran.

But from
The adjoining chamber broke the din of voices,
The clattering tread of armèd men: at times
A shriller cry, that yelled out, "Death to Richelieu!"

Rich.

Speak not of me; thy country is in danger!

Fran.

Baradas
Questioned me close — demurred — until, at last,
O'er-ruled by Orleans, gave the packet — told me
That life and death were in the scroll:
And Orleans promised thousands,
When Bouillon's trumpets in the streets of Paris
Rang out shrill answer: hastening from the house,
My footstep in the stirrup, Marion stole
Across the threshold, whispering, "Lose no moment
Ere Richelieu have the packet: tell him, too,
Murder is in the winds of night, and Orleans
Swears, ere the dawn the Cardinal shall be clay."
She said, and trembling fled within: when lo!
A hand of iron griped me! Thro' the dark,
Gleamed the dim shadow of an armèd man:
Ere I could draw, the prize was wrested from me,
And a hoarse voice gasped — "Spy, I spare thee, for
This steel is virgin to thy lord!" — with that
He vanished. — Scared and trembling for thy safety,
I mounted, fled, and kneeling at thy feet,
Implore thee to acquit my faith; but not,
Like him, to spare my life.

Rich.

Who spake of life?
I bade thee grasp that packet as thine honour —
A jewel worth whole hecatombs of lives!
Begone! Redeem thine honour! Back to Marion —
Or Baradas — or Orleans: track the robber:
Regain the packet — or crawl on to age —
Age and gray hairs like mine — and know thou hast lost
That which had made thee great and saved thy country.
See me not till thou hast bought the right to see me.
Away! Nay, cheer thee! thou hast not failed yet
There 's no such word as "fail!"

Fran.

Bless you, my lord,
For that one smile! I 'll wear it on my heart
To light me back to triumph."⁹   [*Exit François.* L.

Rich.

The poor youth!
An elder had asked life.   I love the young:
For as great men live not in their own time
But in the age to come, so in the young my soul
Makes many Richelieus.   He will win it yet.
François?   He 's gone.   My murder;   Marion's warning;
This bravo's threat: O for the morrow's dawn!
I 'll set my spies to work — I 'll make all space,
As does the sun, an universal eye.
Huguet shall track — Joseph confess — ha! ha!
Strange, while I laughed I shuddered, and e'en now
Thro' the chill air the beating of my heart
Sounds like the death-watch by a sick man's pillow.
If Huguet could deceive me!   [*Listens.   Noise outside.*
Hoofs without—
The gates unclose — steps, near and nearer!
                                   [*Enter Julie de Mortemar* L.

Julie.

Cardinal!   My father!   *Falls at his feet.*

Rich.

Julie! at this hour; and in tears.
What ails thee?

Julie.

I am safe with thee!

Rich.

Safe! why in all the storms of this wide world
What wind would mar the violet?

Julie.

That man—
Why did I love him? — clinging to a breast
That knows no shelter?
Listen: late at noon—
The marriage-day — ev'n then no more a lover,
He left me coldly.   Well, I sought my chamber
To weep and wonder; but to hope and dream:
Sudden a mandate from the king,— to attend
Forthwith his pleasure at the Louvre.

Rich.

Ha!
You did obey the summons; and the king
Reproached your hasty nuptials.

Julie.

Were that all!
He frowned and chid; proclaimed the bond unlawful;
Bade me not quit my chamber in the palace :
And there at night — alone — this night! all still,
He sought my presence — dared! — thou read'st the heart,
Read mine: I cannot speak it!

Rich.

He, a king!
You — woman; well, you yielded!

Julie.

Cardinal!
Dare you say "yielded?" Humbled and abashed,
He from the chamber crept: this mighty Louis;
Crept like a baffled felon! — yielded! Ah!
More royalty in woman's honest heart
Than dwells within the crownèd majesty
And sceptered anger of a hundred kings!
Yielded! Heavens! — yielded!

Rich.

To my breast, — close — close!
The world would never need a Richelieu, if
Men — bearded, mailèd men — the lords of earth —
Resisted flattery, falsehood, avarice, pride,
As this poor child, with the dove's innocent scorn,
Her sex's tempters, vanity and power!
He left you — well!

Julie.

Then came a sharper trial!
At the king's suit, the Count de Baradas
Sought me, to soothe, to fawn, to flatter, while
On his smooth lip insult appeared more hateful

7

For the false mask of pity: letting fall
Dark hints of treachery, with a world of sighs
That heaven had granted to so base a lord
The heart whose coldest friendship were to him
What Mexico to misers!   Stung at last
By my disdain, the dim and glimmering sense
Of his cloaked words broke into bolder light;
And then—ah! then, my haughty spirit failed me;
Then I was weak—wept—O! such bitter tears!
For (turn thy face aside, and let me whisper
The horror to thine ear) then I did learn
That he—that Adrian—that my husband— knew
The king's polluting suit and deemed it honour!
Then all the terrible and loathsome truth
Glared on me; coldness, waywardness, reserve,
Mystery of looks, words—all unravelled, and
I saw the impostor where I had loved the god.

Rich.

I think thou wrongest thy husband—but proceed.

Julie.

Did you say " wronged " him?   Cardinal, my father,
Did you say " wronged?"   Prove it! and life shall glow
One prayer for thy reward and his forgiveness.

Rich.

Let me know all.

Julie.

To the despair he caused
The courtier left me; but amid the chaos
Darted one guiding ray—to 'scape—to fly—
Reach Adrian, learn the worst: 't was then near midnight;
Trembling, I left my chamber; sought the queen;
Fell at her feet; revealed the unholy peril;
Implored her aid to flee our joint disgrace:
Moved, she embraced and soothed me; nay, preserved.
Her words sufficed to unlock the palace gates;

I hastened home — but home was desolate —
No Adrian there! Fearing the worst, I fled
To thee, directed hither. As my wheels
Paused at thy gates, the clang of arms behind
The ring of hoofs ——

Rich.

'T was but my guards, fair trembler. [*Aside.*
So Huguet keeps his word, my omens wronged him.

Julie.

O, in one hour what years of anguish crowd !

Rich.

Nay, there 's no danger now. Thou need'st rest.
Come, thou shalt lodge beside me. Tush ! be cheered !
My rosiest Amazon, thou wrong'st thy Theseus.
All will be well yet ; yet all well.
    [*During this speech the moonlight fades away, and
      the scene is darkened.*
    [*Exeunt* L. U. E. *Enter Huguet* L. I. E. *and De
      Mauprat, in complete armour, his visor down.*

Hug.

Not here !

De Maup.

O, I will find him; fear not: hence and guard
The galleries where the menials sleep; plant sentries
At every outlet. Chance should throw no shadow
Between the vengeance and the victim! Go!
· Ere yon brief vapour that obscures the moon,
As doth our deed pale conscience, pass away,
The mighty shall be ashes.

Hug.

Will you not
A second arm ?

De Maup.

To slay one weak old man ?
Away! No lesser wrongs than mine can make
This murder lawful. Hence!

Hug.

A short farewell!

    [*Exit Huguet* L. I. E.   *Enter Richelieu,* L. U. F. *not*
      perceiving De Mauprat.

Rich.

How heavy is the air! the vestal lamp
Of the sad moon, weary with vigil, dies
In the still temple of the solemn heaven.
The very darkness lends itself to fear —
To treason ——

De Maup.

And to death!

Rich.

Ha!
What art thou, wretch?

De Maup.

Thy doomsman!

Rich.

Ho, my guards!
Huguet! Montbrassil! Vermont!

De Maup.

Ay, thy spirits
Forsake thee, wizard; thy bold men of mail
Are my confederates. Stir not! but one step,
And know the next — thy grave!

Rich.

Thou liest, knave!
I am old, infirm — most feeble — but thou liest!
Armand de Richelieu dies not by the hand
Of man: the stars have said it;[20] and the voice
Of my own prophet and oracular soul
Confirms the shining sybils! Call them all —
Thy brother butchers: earth hath no such fiend —
No! as one parricide of his father-land,
Who dares in Richelieu murder France!

De Maup.

Thy stars
Deceive thee, Cardinal: thy soul of wiles
May against kings and armaments avail,
And mock the embattled world; but powerless now
Against the sword of one resolvèd man,
Upon whose forehead thou hast written shame!
Listen:
In his hot youth, a soldier urged to crime
Against the State, placed in your hands his life;
You did not strike the blow — but o'er his head,
Upon the gossamer thread of your caprice,
Hovered the axe: your death
Had set him free: he purposed not nor prayed it.
One day you summoned — mocked him with smooth
    pardon,
Showered wealth upon him, bade an angel's face
Turn earth to paradise.

Rich.

Well!

De Maup.

Was this mercy?
A Cæsar's generous vengeance?—Cardinal, no!
Judas, not Cæsar, was the model! You
Saved him from death, for shame.
Expect no mercy!
Behold De Mauprat!

                  [*Lifts his visor.*

Rich.

To thy knees, and crawl
For pardon; or, I tell thee, thou shalt live
For such remorse, that, did I hate thee, I
Would bid thee strike, that I might be avenged!
It was to save my Julie from the king,
That in thy valour I forgave thy crime.
It was, when thou — the rash and ready tool,
Yea, of that shame thou loath'st, didst leave thy hearth

To the polluter—in these arms thy bride
Found the protecting shelter thine withheld.
Julie de Mauprat—Julie!

[*Enter Julie* L. U. E.

Lo! my witness, sir!

De Maup.

What marvel's this?—I dream! My Julie—thou!

Julie.

Henceforth all bond
Between us twain is broken. Were it not
For this old man, I might, in truth, have lost
The right—now mine—to scorn thee.

Rich.

You hear her, sir.

De Maup.

Thou, with some slander, hast her sense infected!

Julie.

No, sir; he did excuse thee in despite
Of all that wears the face of truth. Thy friend—
Thy confidant—familiar—Baradas—
Himself revealed thy baseness.

De Maup.

Baseness!

Rich.

Ay;
That thou didst court dishonour.

De Maup.

Baradas!
Where is thy thunder, Heaven? Duped! snared! un-
done!
Thou—thou couldst not believe him! Thou dost love
me!

Julie.

Love him!   Ah!
Be still, my heart!   Love you I did: how fondly,
Woman — if women were my listeners now —
Alone could tell!   Forever fled my dream:
Farewell — all's over!

Rich.

Nay, my daughter, these
Are but the blinding mists of day-break love
Sprung from its very heat, and heralding
A noon of happy summer.   Take her hand
And speak the truth with which your heart runs over —
That this Count Judas, this incarnate falsehood,
Never lied more than when he told thy Julie
That Adrian loved her not — except, indeed,
When he told Adrian Julie could betray him.

Julie.   [*Embracing De Mauprat.*

You love me, then! you love me! and they wronged you!

De Maup.

Ah, couldst thou doubt?

Rich.

Why, man, the very mole   •
Less blind than thou!   Baradas loves thy wife:
Had hoped her hand; hopes even now
To make thy corse his footstool to thy bed.
Where was thy wit, man ?   Ho! these schemes are glass!
The very sun shines through them.

De Maup.

O, my lord,   [*Kneels.*
Can you forgive me ?

Rich.

Ay, and save you!

De Maup.

Save! —
Terrible word!   O, save thyself! these halls
Swarm with thy foes: already for thy blood
Pants thirsty murder!

Julie.

Murder!

Rich.

Hush! put by
The woman.   Hush! a shriek — a cry — a breath
Too loud would startle from its horrent pause
The swooping death!   Go to the door and listen!
Now for escape!

                              [Julie goes to door L.

De Maup.

None — none!   Their blades shall pass
This heart to thine.

                  Rich.·   *[Dryly.* '

An honourable outwork,
But much too near the citadel.   I think
That I can trust you now.

          [Slowly, and gazing on him intently.

Yes: I will trust you.
How many of my troop league with you?

De Maup.

All! —
We are your troop!

                Rich.

And Huguet?

De Maup.

Is our captain.

                Rich.

Retributive Power!
This comes of spies.
All?   The lion's skin too short to-night;
Now for the fox's.

                Julie.

A hoarse gathering murmur!
Hurrying and heavy footsteps!

                Rich.

Ha! the posterns!

De Maup.

No egress where no sentry!

Rich.

I have it! to my chamber—quick!   Come, Julie!
Hush! Mauprat come!

Voices Outside.

Death to the Cardinal!

Rich.

We will
Baffle them yet.

    [*Exeunt De Mauprat, Julie, and Richelieu* C.

Hug.   [*Speaking outside.*

This way—this way!

    [*Enter, in eager haste, Huguet and the Conspira-
tors* L. *De Mauprat, appearing, throws back
curtains* C. *disclosing Richelieu upon his bed, and
apparently dead.*

De Maup.

Live the king!
Richelieu is dead!

Omnes.

Dead!

De Maup.

I watched him till he slept.
Heed me.   No trace of blood reveals the deed:
Strangled in sleep: his health had long been broken:
Found breathless in his bed.   So runs our tale;
Remember!   Back to Paris: Orleans gives
Ten thousand crowns, and Baradas a lordship,
To him who first gluts vengeance with the news
That Richelieu is in heaven!   Quick, that all France
May share your joy!

Hug.

I shall be noble!

8

De Maup.

Away.

Omnes.

To horse! to horse!

[*Exeunt Conspirators* L.   *As they throng out De Mauprat goes to Richelieu, who leaps up and exclaims:*

Rich.

Bloodhounds, I laugh at you!

QUICK CURTAIN.

Act Fourth.

Scene First. { PARIS. THE GARDENS OF THE LOUVRE. ORLEANS, BARADAS, DE BERINGHEN, COURTIERS, etc., DISCOVERED.

Orl.

How does my brother bear the Cardinal's death?

Bar.

With grief when thinking on the toils of State;
With joy when thinking on the eyes of Julie.
At times he sighs, " Who now shall govern France?"
Anon exclaims, "Who now shall baffle Louis?"
                    [*Enter Louis XIII. and Courtiers* R. U. E.

Orl.

Now, my liege, now I can embrace a brother.

Louis.

Dear Gaston, yes.   I do believe you love me:
Richelieu denied it—severed us too long.
A great man, Gaston!   Who shall govern France?

Bar.

Yourself, my liege.   That swart and potent star
Eclipsed your royal orb.   He served the country;
But did he serve, or seek to sway, the king?

Louis.

You 're right — he was an able politician, [21]
That 's all.
He was most disloyal in that marriage.
[*Querulously.*]   He knew that Julie pleased me :—a clear proof
He never loved me!

Bar.

O, most clear ! But now
No bar between the lady and your will.
This writ makes all secure : a week or two
                              [*Shows a paper.*
In the Bastile will sober Mauprat's love,
And leave him eager to dissolve a Hymen
That brings him such a home.

Louis.

See to it, count.
                              [*Exit Baradas* R. I. E.
I 'll summon Julie back. A word with you. [*To Orleans.*
          [*King Louis takes aside Orleans, and passes, con-
          versing, through the gardens, followed by court-
          iers* L. U. E. *Enter François.*

Fran.

All search, as yet, in vain for Mauprat : not
At home since yesternoon : a soldier told me
He saw him pass this way with hasty strides :
Should he meet Baradas they 'd rend it from him :
Benignant fortune smile upon me :
I am thy son : if thou desert'st me now,
Come death and snatch me from disgrace.
                              [*Enter De Mauprat* C.

De Maup.

O, let me —
Let me but meet him foot to foot — I'll dig
The Judas from his heart ; albeit the king
Should o'er him cast the purple!

Fran.

Mauprat ! hold :
Where is the——

De Maup.

Well ! What wouldst thou ?

Fran.

The dispatch!
The packet.   Look on me — I serve the Cardinal —
You know me.   Did you not keep guard last night
By Marion's house ?

De Maup.

I did: — no matter now!
They told me he was here!

Fran.

O joy! quick — quick —
The packet thou didst wrest from me?

De Maup.

The packet?
What — art thou he I deemed the Cardinal's spy,
(Dupe that I was) and overhearing Marion —

Fran.

The same — restore it! haste!

De Maup.

I have it not:
Methought it but revealed our scheme to Richelieu.
                    [*Enter Baradas* R. I. E.
Stand back!
Now, villain! now I have thee!
Hence, sir!   [*To François.*
Draw!   [*To Baradas.*
                    Fran.

Art mad? the king's at hand! leave him to Richelieu.
Speak; the dispatch; to whom ——

De Maup.

     [*Dashing François aside and rushing upon
          Baradas.*
Thou triple slanderer!
I'll set my heel upon thy crest!
                    , [*Mauprat and Baradas fight.*

Fran.

Fly—fly! The king!
[*Enter Louis, Orleans, De Beringhen, courtiers and
    guards* L. U. E.

Louis.

Swords drawn before our very palace!
Have our laws died with Richelieu?

Bar.

Pardon, sire,—
My crime but self-defence.²² [*Aside to Louis.*] It is
    De Mauprat!

Louis.

Dare he thus brave us?
[*Baradas goes to the guard and gives writ to the
    Captain.*

De Maup. [*To Louis.*

Sire, in the Cardinal's name——

Bar. [*To Captain.*

Seize him! disarm! to the Bastile!
[*De Mauprat is seized. The Cardinal's march is
    heard. Then enter Richelieu and Joseph, fol-
    lowed by the Cardinal's guard* c.

De Maup. [*To Richelieu.*

Priest and hero—for you are both—
Protect the truth. [*De Mauprat kneels.*

Rich.

What is this? [*Takes writ.*

All.

The Cardinal!

Bar. [*In consternation.*

The dead returned to life!

Louis.

What! A *mock* death! this tops
The infinite of insult.

De Ber. [*Aside.*

Fact in philosophy : foxes have got
Nine lives, as well as cats!

Bar.

Be firm, my liege.

Louis.

I have assumed the sceptre; I will wield it!

Jos. [*Aside.*

The tide runs counter; there 'll be shipwreck somewhere.
[*Baradas and Orleans keep close to the king—
     whispering and prompting him, while Richelieu
     speaks.*

Rich.

High treason! Faviaux! still that stale pretence.
My liege, bad men (ay, count, most knavish men!)
Abuse your royal goodness. For this soldier,
France hath none braver: and his youth's hot folly,
Misled—by whom your highness may conjecture!—
[*To Orleans.*
Is long since cancelled by a loyal manhood.
I, sire, have pardoned him.

Louis.

And we do give
Your pardon to the winds. Sir, do your duty! [*To officer.*

Rich.

What, sire? You do not know—O, pardon me—
You know not yet, that this brave, honest heart,
Stood between mine and murder! Sire! for my sake—
For your old servant's sake—undo this wrong.
See, let me rend the sentence.
[*Offers as if he would tear the writ.*

Louis.

At your peril!
This is too much.—Again, sir, do your duty! [*To officer.*
[*De Mauprat advances.*

Rich.

Speak not, but go: I would not see young valour
So humbled as grey service.

De Maup.

Fare you well!
Save Julie, and console her.
[*De Mauprat goes up with guard. Richelieu goes*
R. *to Joseph. The courtiers surround Louis,*
who sits L.

Fran. [*Aside to De Mauprat.*

The dispatch!
Your fate, foes, life, hang on a word! to whom?

De Maup.

To Huguet.
[*Exeunt Mauprat and guard* L. U. E.

Bar. [*Aside to François.*

Has he the packet?

Fran. [*Aside to Baradas.*

He will not reveal—
[*Aside.*] Work, brain! beat, heart! "There's no such
word as fail."
[*Exit François* R. U. E.
Rich. [*Fiercely.*

Room, my lords, room! The minister of France
Can need no intercession with the king.
[*Courtiers fall back. The king rises.*

Louis.

What means this false report of death, lord Cardinal?

Rich.

Are you then angered, sire, that I still live?

Louis.

No ; but such artifice —

Rich.

Not mine : look elsewhere.
Louis — my castle swarmed with the assassins.

Bar.   [*Advancing* L.

We have punished them already.   Huguet now
In the Bastile.   O ! my lord, we were prompt
To avenge you — we were——

Rich.

We ?   Ha ! ha ! you hear,
My liege !   What page, man, in the last court grammar
Made you a plural ?[23]   Count, you have seized the hire-
    ling : —
Sire, shall I name the master ?

.   *Louis.*

[*Haughtily, to the Cardinal.*

Enough !
Your eminence must excuse a longer audience.
To your own palace : for our conference, this
Nor place, nor season.

Rich.

Good my liege, for Justice,
All place a temple, and all season, summer !
Do you deny me justice ?   Saints of heaven !
He turns from me !   Do you deny me justice ?
My liege, my Louis,
Do you refuse me justice — audience even —
In the pale presence of the baffled Murder ?[24]   [*All start.*

Louis.

Lord Cardinal, one by one you have severed from me
The bonds of human love ; all near and dear
Marked out for vengeance, exile, or the scaffold.
You find me now amidst my trustiest friends,
My closest kindred ; you would tear them from me ;

9

They murder you forsooth, since me they love.
Enough of plots and treasons for one reign !
Home ! home ! my lord, and sleep away these phantoms !
                    [*Louis and courtiers cross* R.

Rich.

Sire !
I — patience, heaven ! sweet heaven ! Sire, from the foot
Of that great throne, these hands have raised aloft
On an Olympus, looking down on mortals
And worshipped by their awe — before the foot
Of that high throne, spurn you the grey-haired man,
Who gave you empire, and now sues for safety ?

Louis.

No : — when we see your eminence in truth
At the foot of the throne, we 'll listen to you.
                    [*Exit Louis followed by all the Courtiers* R.

            Orl.   [*As he goes out.*

Saved !

            Bar.   [*As he goes out.*

For this, deep thanks to Julie and to Mauprat !

Jos.

If you had been less haughty ——.

Rich.

No time for ifs and buts !
I will accuse these traitors.
François shall witness that De Baradas
Gave him the secret missive for De Bouillon,
And told him life and death were in the scroll.
I will — I will !

Jos.

Tush ! François is your creature ;
So they will say, and laugh at you : your witness
Must be that same dispatch.

Rich.

Away to Marion!

Jos.

I have been there: she is seized, removed, imprisoned,
By the count's orders.

Rich.

Goddess of bright dreams,
My country, shalt thou lose me now, when most
Thou need'st thy worshipper?   My native land!
Let me but ward this dagger from thy heart,
And die but on thy bosom!

[*Enter Julie* C.

Julie.

Heaven, I thank thee!
It cannot be, or this all-powerful
Would not stand idly thus.

Rich.

What dost thou here?
Home!

Julie.

Home?   Is Adrian there? you 're dumb, yet strive
For words; I see them trembling on your lip,
But choked by pity.   It was truth — all truth!
Seized — the Bastile — and in your presence, too!
Cardinal, where is Adrian?   Think! he saved
Your life: your name is infamy, if wrong
Should come to his!

Rich.

Be soothed, child.

Julie.

Child no more;
I love, and I am woman!   Hope and suffer:
Love, suffering, hope — what else doth make the strength
And majesty of woman?   Let thine eyes meet mine:

Answer me but one word: I am a wife:
I ask thee for my home, my fate, my all—
Where is my husband?

Rich.

You are Richelieu's ward;
A soldier's bride: they who insist on truth
Must outface fear: you ask me for your husband?
There—where the clouds of heaven look darkest, o'er
The domes of the Bastile!²⁵

Julie.

O, mercy! mercy!
Save him, restore him, father! Art thou not
The Cardinal-king? the lord of life and death—
Beneath whose light, as deeps beneath the moon,
The solemn tides of empire ebb and flow?—
Art thou not Richelieu?

Rich.

Yesterday I was!—
To-day a very weak old man: to-morrow,
I know not what!   [*Crosses to* L.
              Julie.   [*To Joseph.*

Do you conceive his meaning?
Alas! I cannot. But, methinks my senses
Are duller than they were.

'   *Jos.*

The king is chafed
Against his servant. Lady, while we speak,
The lackey of the ante-room is not
More powerless than the minister of France.
        [*Joseph goes to Richelieu. Enter First Courtier* R.

First Cour.

Madame de Mauprat!
Pardon, your eminence—even now I seek
This lady's home, commanded by the king
To pray her presence.

Julie.　　　[*Clinging to Richelieu.*

Think of my dead father!
Think, how, an infant, clinging to your knees,
And looking to your eyes, the wrinkled care
Fled from your brow before the smile of childhood,
Fresh from the dews of heaven! Think of this,
And take me to your breast.

Rich.　　　[*To Courtier.*

To those who sent you!
And say you found the virtue they would slay,
Here—couched upon this heart, as at an altar,
And sheltered by the wings of sacred Rome!
Begone!　　　[*The Courtier uncovers and bows reverently.*

First Cour.

My lord, I am your friend and servant.
Misjudge me not; but never yet was Louis
So roused against you: shall I take this answer?—
It were to be your foe.
　　　　　　Rich.
All time my foe,
If I, a priest, could cast this holy sorrow
Forth from her last asylum!
　　　[*Exit First Courtier* R. *Julie faints in the Cardinal's arms.*

Rich.

God help thee, child! She hears not! Look upon her!
Her father loved me so! and in that age
When friends are brothers; she has been to me
Soother, nurse, plaything, daughter. Are these tears?[26]
O! shame! shame! dotage!
　　　[*Joseph assists to place Julie on seat* L.

Jos.

Tears are not for eyes
That rather need the lightning, which can pierce
Through barrèd gates and triple walls, to smite
Crime, where it cowers in secret! The dispatch!

Set every spy to work ; the morrow's sun
Must see that written treason in your hands,
Or rise upon your ruin.
                              Rich.

Ay — and close upon my corse.
Yes ! to-morrow, triumph or death.
Look up, child!   Lead us, Joseph.
        [*As they are going* c., *enter Baradas and De Ber-
            inghen* R.
                              Bar.

My lord, the king cannot believe your eminence
So far forgets your duty, and his greatness,
As to resist his mandate.   Pray you, madam,
Obey the king: no cause for fear.

                Julie.   [*To Richelieu.*
My father!
                Rich.   [*To Baradas.*
She shall not stir!
                Bar.
You are not of her kindred —
An orphan ——
                Rich.
The country is her mother!
                Bar.
The country is the king!
                Rich.
Ay, is it so;
Then wakes the power, which in the age of iron ²⁷
Burst forth to curb the great, and raise the low.
Mark where she stands: [*He places Julie* L. C.
Around her form I draw
The awful circle ²⁸ of our solemn church!
                [*Baradas and De Beringhen uncover.*
Set but a foot within that holy ground,
And on thy head — yea, though it wore a crown —
I launch the curse of Rome!
            [*All but Richelieu and Joseph kneel.   Joseph dis-
                plays the cross.*

Bar. [*Rises.*

I dare not brave you!
I do but speak the orders of my king.
The church, your rank, power, very word, my lord,
Suffice you for resistance: blame yourself,
If it should cost you power!

Rich.

That my stake.   Ah!
Dark gamester! what is thine!   Look to it well!
Lose not a trick.   By this same hour to-morrow
Thou shalt have France, or I thy head!

Bar.   [*Aside to De Beringhen.*

He cannot have the dispatch ?

Jos.   [*Aside.*

Patience!   Patience!

Rich.

O! monk!
Leave patience to the saints — for I am human!
Did not thy father die for France, poor orphan!
[*To Julie, embracing her.*
And now they say thou hast no father.   Fie!
Art thou not pure and good ?   If so, thou art
A part of that — the beautiful, the sacred —
Which, in all climes, men that have hearts adore
By the great title of their mother country.

Bar.

He wanders !

Rich.

So; cling close unto my breast:
Here where thou droop'st lies France!   I am very feeble:
Of little use it seems to either now.
Well, well — we will go home.

Bar.

In sooth, my lord,
You do need rest; the burdens of the state
O'ertask your health.

Rich.   [*To Joseph.*

I'm patient, see!

Bar.

His mind
And life are breaking fast.

Rich.   [*Overhearing him.*

Irreverent ribald!
If so, beware the falling ruins!   Hark!
I tell thee, scorner of these whitening hairs,
When this snow melteth there shall come a flood!
Avaunt! my name is Richelieu — I defy thee!
Walk blindfold on: behind thee stalks the headsman.
Ha! ha! — how pale he glares!   Heaven save my country!
                          [*Falls back in Joseph's arms.*

CURTAIN.

Act Fifth.

Bar.

All smiles: the Cardinal's swoon of yesterday
Heralds his death to-day: could he survive,
It would not be as minister—so great
The king's resentment at the priest's defiance.
All smiles! and yet should this accursed De Mauprat
Have given our packet to another—'Sdeath!
I dare not think of it!

Orl.

You 've sent to search him?

Bar.

Sent, sir, to search?—that hireling hands may find
Upon him, naked, with its broken seal,
That scroll whose every word is death?   No—no—
These hands alone must clutch that awful secret.
I dare not leave the palace, night or day,
While Richelieu lives: his minions, creatures, spies—
Not one must reach the king.

Orl.

What hast thou done?

Bar.

Summoned De Mauprat hither.

Orl.

Could this Huguet,
Who prayed thy presence with so fierce a fervour,
Have thieved the scroll?

10

Bar. *

Huguet was housed with us,
The very moment we dismissed the courier.
It cannot be: a stale trick for reprieve.
But, to make sure, I've sent our trustiest friend
To see and sift him.   Hist! here comes the king.
How fare you, sire?

[*Enter Louis* c.

Louis.

In the same mind I have
Decided: yes, he would forbid your presence,
My brother,—yours, my friend: then, Julie, too:
Thwarts—braves—defies—

[*Suddenly turning to Baradas.*

We make you minister.
Gaston, for you—the baton of our armies.
You love me, do you not?

Orl.

O, love you, sire!
[*Aside.*] Never so much as now.

Bar.

May I deserve
Your trust [*aside*]—until you sign your abdication.
My liege, but one way left to daunt De Mauprat,
And Julie to divorce. —We must prepare
The death-writ: what, tho' signed and sealed? we can
Withhold the enforcement.

Louis.

Ah, you may prepare it:
We need not urge it to effect.

Bar.

Exactly!
No haste, my liege.   [*Aside.*]   He may live one hour
longer.

[*Enter Courtier* c.

Cour.

The Lady Julie, sire, implores an audience.

Louis.

Aha! repentant of her folly!— Well,
Admit her.

Bar.

Sire, she comes for Mauprat's pardon.
And the conditions——

Louis.

You are minister,
We leave to you our answer.
    [*The Captain of the Guard enters* L. *and whispers
      to Baradas, who has advanced to meet him.*

Capt.

The Chevalier
De Mauprat waits below.

Bar.   [*Aside.*

Now the dispatch!
    [*Exeunt Baradas and Captain* L. *Enter Julie* C.

Julie.

My liege, you sent for me. I come where grief
Should come when guiltless, while the name of king
Is holy on the earth. Here, at the feet
Of power, I kneel for mercy.

Louis.

Mercy, Julie,
Is an affair of state. The Cardinal should
In this be your interpreter.

Julie.

Alas!
I know not if that mighty spirit now
Stoops to the things of earth. Nay, while I speak,
Perchance he hears the orphan by the throne

Where kings themselves need pardon. — O, my liege,
Be father to the fatherless: in you
Dwells my last hope.

[Enter Baradas L.

Bar. *[Aside.*

He has not the dispatch;
Smiled while we searched, and braves me.

Louis. *[Gently.*

What wouldst thou?

Julie.

A single life. You reign o'er millions; what
Is one man's life to you? and yet to me
'T is France — 't is earth — 't is everything! — a life,
A human life — my husband's.

Louis.

[Aside to Baradas, who has quietly approached R.

Speak to her.
I am not marble: give her hope — or —— *[Exit Louis* C.

Bar. *[To Julie.*

Madam,
Vex not your king, whose heart, too soft for justice,
Leaves to his ministers that solemn charge.

Julie.

You were his friend.

Bar.

I was, before I loved thee.

Julie.

Loved me!

Bar.

Hush, Julie! couldst thou misinterpret
My acts, thoughts, motives, nay, my very words,
Here — in this palace?

Julie.

Now I know I 'm mad:
Even that memory failed me.

Bar.

I am young,
Well-born and brave as Mauprat: — for thy sake
I peril what he has not — fortune — power;
All to great souls most dazzling.   I alone
Can save thee from thy tyrant, now my puppet.
Be mine : annul the mockery of this marriage,
And, on the day I clasp thee to my breast,
De Mauprat shall be free.

Julie.

Thou durst not speak
Thus in his ear !
          [*Pointing to Louis, who is seen, passing, at back,
               with Orleans.*
Thou double traitor ! — tremble !
I will unmask thee.

Bar.

I will say thou ravest.
And, see this scroll: its letters shall be blood!
Go to the king, count with me word for word:
And while you pray the life — I write the sentence !
                              [*Goes to table* R.

Julie.

Stay, stay.   [*Rushing to the king, who enters* C.
You have a kind and princely heart,
Tho' sometimes it is silent: you were born
To power — it has not flushed you into madness,
As it doth meaner men.   Banish my husband —
Dissolve our marriage — cast me to that grave
Of human ties, where hearts congeal to ice,
In the dark convent's everlasting winter
(Surely eno' for justice, hate, revenge),
But spare this life, thus lonely, scathed, and bloomless;
And when thou stand'st for judgment on thine own,
The deed shall shine beside thee as an angel.

Louis.   [*Much affected.*

Go, go, to Baradas: and annul thy marriage,
And——

Julie.

[*Anxiously, and watching his countenance.*
Be his bride?

Louis.

A form, a mere decorum;
Thou know'st I love thee.

Julie.

O, thou sea of shame,
And not one star.
    [*The king goes up the stage, and passes out* C.
    in evident emotion.

Bar.   [*Advances.*

Well, thy election, Julie:
This hand—his grave!

Julie.

His grave! and I——

Bar.

Can save him.
Swear to be mine.

Julie.

That were a bitterer death!
Avaunt, thou tempter! I did ask his life
A boon, and not the barter of dishonour.
The heart can break, and scorn you: wreak your malice;
Adrian and I will leave you this sad earth,
And pass together hand in hand to heaven.

Bar.

You have decided. Listen to me, lady:
I am no base intriguer. I adored thee
From the first glance of those inspiring eyes:
With thee entwined ambition, hope, the future.

I will not lose thee!   I can place thee nearest—
Ay, to the throne—nay, on the throne, perchance:
My star is at its zenith.   Look upon me;
Hast thou decided?

Julie.

No, no; you can see
How weak I am; be human, sir—one moment.

Bar.

[*Signals by stamping.   Enter De Mauprat, with
guards* L.

Behold thy husband: shall he pass to death,
And know thou couldst have saved him?

Julie.

Adrian, speak!
But say you wish to live!—if not your wife
Your slave: do with me as you will!

De Maup.

Once more!—
Why this is mercy, count!   O, think, my Julie,
Life, at the best, is short—but love immortal!

Bar.   [*Taking Julie's hand.*

Ah, loveliest——

Julie.

Go! that touch has made me iron!
We have decided—death!

Bar.   [*To De Mauprat.*

Now, say to whom
Thou gavest the packet, and thou yet shalt live.

De Maup.

I 'll tell thee nothing.

Bar.

Hark,—the rack!

De Maup.

Thy penance
Forever, wretch`!—What rack is like the conscience ?

Bar.

Hence to the headsman!

[*Enter a Page* c. *He announces :*

Page.

His Eminence, the Cardinal, Duc de Richelieu.
[*Enter Richelieu* c., *pale, feeble, leaning on Joseph,*
attended by gentlemen, pages, etc., and followed by
three secretaries of state, with papers.

Julie. [*Rushing to Richelieu.*

You live—you live—and Adrian shall not die!

Rich.

Not if an old man's prayers, himself near death,
Can aught avail thee, daughter! Count, you now
[*To Baradas.*
Hold what I held on earth:—one boon, my lord,
This soldier's life.

Bar.

The stake—my head!—you said it.
I cannot lose one trick. Remove your prisoner.
[*To officer.*

Julie.

No!—No!—

[*Enter Louis and Courtiers* c.

Rich. [*To officer.*

Hold, sir.

[*To the king.*

My liege,
Your worn-out servant, willing to spare you
Some pain of conscience, would forestall your wishes:
I do resign my office.

De Maup.

You!

Julie.

All 's over.

Rich.

My end draws near.   These sad ones, sire, I love them:
I do not ask his life ; but suffer justice
To halt, until I can dismiss his soul,
Charged with an old man's blessing.

Louis.

Surely!

Bar.

Sire——

Louis.

Silence: small favour to a dying servant.

. *Rich.*

You would consign your armies to the baton
Of your most honoured brother.   Sire, so be it.
Your minister, the Count de Baradas;
A most sagacious choice!   Your secretaries
Of state attend me, sire, to render up
The ledgers of a realm.— I do beseech you,
Suffer these noble gentlemen to learn
The nature of the glorious task that waits them,
Here, in my presence.

Louis.

You say well, my lord.
          [*To secretaries, as he seats himself on throne.*
Approach, sirs.
                    [*The secretaries advance and kneel.*

Rich.

I — I — faint!— air — air —
                    [*De Mauprat assists Richelieu to a sofa* L.
I thank you: draw near, my children.

II

Bar.

He's too weak to question;
Nay, scarce to speak; all's safe.

> [*Julie kneels beside the Cardinal. Joseph stands
> near Richelieu, watching the king. Baradas
> near the king's chair. A page takes papers from
> the secretaries and gives them to Louis.*

First Sec.

The affairs of Portugal,
Most urgent, sire:—One short month since the Duc
Braganza was a rebel.

Louis.

And is still.

First Sec.

No, sire; he has succeeded; he is now
Crowned king of Portugal; craves instant succour
Against the arms of Spain.

Louis.

> [*Louis looks carelessly at papers and gives them to
> Baradas.*

We will not grant it
Against his lawful king. Eh, count?

Bar.

No, sire.

First Sec.

But Spain's your deadliest foe: whatever
Can weaken Spain must strengthen France. The Car-
    dinal
Would send the succours;—balance, sire, of Europe!

Louis.

The Cardinal! balance! We'll consider. Eh, count?

Bar.

Yes, sire: [*To Secretary*] fall back.

First Sec.

But ——

Bar.

O ! fall back, sir.

[*Secretary rises, and retires.*

Jos.

Humph !

Second Sec.

The affairs of England, sire, most urgent : Charles
The First has lost a battle that decides
One-half his realm; craves moneys, sire, and succour.

Louis.

He shall have both.— Eh, Baradas ?

Bar.

Yes, sire.
O that dispatch! — my veins are fire !

Rich.

[*Feebly, but with great distinctness.*

My liege,
Forgive me; Charles's cause is lost : a man,
Named Cromwell, risen : a great man! your succour
Would fail; your loans be squandered!   Pause : reflect.

Louis.

Reflect.   Eh, Baradas ?

Bar.

Reflect, sire.

Jos.

Humph !

Louis.   [*Aside.*

I half repent !   No successor to Richelieu.
Round me thrones totter; dynasties dissolve:
The soil he guards alone escapes the earthquake.

Jos.

Our star not yet eclipsed: you mark the king?
O had we the dispatch!

Rich.

Ah! Joseph!—child—
Would I could help thee!

Bar. [*To Secretary.*

Sir, fall back.

Second Sec.

But——

Bar.

Pshaw, sir!

[*Secretary retires.*

Third Sec.

The secret correspondence, sire, most urgent:
Accounts of spies; deserters; heretics;
Poisoners; schemes against yourself.

Louis.

Myself! most urgent!
[*Louis looks at this document eagerly. Enter François* c. *He passes behind the Cardinal's attendants, and, sheltered by them from the sight of
Baradas, gives packet to Richelieu.*

Fran.

My lord!
I have not failed!

Rich.

Hush!

[*Opens packet and looks at its contents.*

Third Sec. [*To the king.*

Sire, the Spaniards
Have reinforced their army on the frontiers.
The Duc de Bouillon——

Rich.

Hold! [*Secretary retires.*]   In this department, [*To Louis.*
A paper: here, sire, read yourself; then take
The count's advice in 't.

> [*François takes packet and gives it to the king,*
> *who rises and goes* L.   *At same time enter De*
> *Beringhen hastily, draws aside Baradas, and*
> *whispers to him.*

Bar.

> [*Starting wildly away from De Beringhen.*
What! and reft it from thee?
Ha!—hold!

> [*Tries to intercept delivery of the packet.*

Jos.   [*To Baradas.*

Fall back, son.   It is your turn now!

Bar.

Death!—the dispatch!

Louis.   [*Reading.*

To Bouillon—and signed Orleans!
Baradas, too: league with our foes of Spain!
Capture the king!—Saints of heaven!
These are the men I loved!

> [*Richelieu falls back, feeble and fainting.*

Jos.

See to the Cardinal!

Bar.

He's dying! and I yet shall dupe the king.

Louis.   [*Rushing to Richelieu.*

Richelieu!   Lord Cardinal! 't is I resign!
Reign thou!

Jos.

Alas! too late!—he faints!

Louis.

Reign, Richelieu!

Rich. [*Feebly.*

With absolute power?

Louis.

Most absolute! — O, live!
If not for me — for France!

Rich. [*With more animation.*

France!

Louis.

O! this treason!
The army — Orleans — Bouillon — Heaven! the Span-
iard!
Where will they be next week?

[*As Louis turns toward the throne* c. *he encounters
Baradas, kneeling; he motions him away and
falls into his seat. Baradas rises and goes to* R.

Rich.

[*Starting up, and with force.*

There, — at my feet!

[*All show amazement at Richelieu's recovery.*
[*To First and Second Secretaries.*

Ere the clock strike — the envoys have their answer!

[*First and Second Secretaries exeunt.*
[*To Third Secretary, with a ring.*

This to De Chavigny: he knows the rest:
No need of parchment here: he must not halt
For sleep — for food. — In my name, — mine — he will
Arrest the Duc de Bouillon at the head
Of his army! — Ho! there, Count de Baradas,

[*Exit Third Secretary.*

Thou hast lost the stake! — Away with him! [29]

[*Baradas draws sword; attempts to rush out; is
arrested; throws down sword; bows to the
king; and goes out guarded.*

Embrace your husband! [*To Julie.*

[*De Mauprat and Julie embrace.*

At last the old man blesses you!

Louis.   [*Peevishly.*

One moment makes a startling cure, lord Cardinal. [30]

Rich.

Yes, Sire, for in that moment there did pass
Into this withered frame the might of France!
My own dear France! I have thee yet: I have saved
    thee!
I clasp thee still! it was thy voice that called me
Back from the tomb! What mistress like our country?

Louis.

For Mauprat's pardon — well! But Julie,— Richelieu:
Leave me one thing to love!

Rich.

A subject's luxury:
Yet, if you must love something, sire — love me!

Louis.

          [*Smiling, in spite of himself.*
Fair proxy for a young, fresh demoiselle!

Rich.

Your heart speaks for my clients : — kneel, my children,
And thank your king —
         [*De Mauprat and Julie kneel. De Beringhen
           attempts to go out* c., *but is met by Joseph, who
           prevents him.*
               Louis.
Rise — rise — be happy.
         [*De Beringhen advances and speaks.*

De Ber.   [*Falteringly.*

My lord — you are most happily recovered.

Rich.

But you are pale, dear Beringhen: this air
Suits not your delicate frame: I long have thought so:
Sleep not another night in Paris: go,—
Or else your precious life may be in danger.
Leave France, dear Beringhen.   [*Orleans kneels to Louis.*

De Ber.

St. Denis travelled without his head!
Faith, I'm luckier than St. Denis!
I shall have time,
More than I asked for, to discuss the pâté.
                         [*Exit De Beringhen* C.

Rich.   [*To Orleans.*

For you, repentance, absence and confession.
          [*Orleans goes out* C.   *To François, who kneels* L.
Never say fail again.   Brave boy!
                         [*To Joseph* L.

He'll be —   •
A bishop first.

Jos.

Ah, Cardinal —

Rich.

Ah, Joseph.
          [*To Louis, as De Mauprat and Julie converse
              apart.*
See, my liege, through plots and counterplots,
Through gain and loss, through glory and disgrace,
Along the plains where passionate discord rears
Eternal Babel, still the holy stream
Of human happiness glides on.

Louis.

And must we
Thank, for that also, our prime minister?

Rich.

No—let us own it:—there is One above
Sways the harmonious mystery of the world
Better than prime ministers.

CURTAIN.

RICHELIEU.

I.—THE DRAMA AND CHARACTER OF RICHELIEU.

"RICHELIEU" stands in the front rank of romantic dramas. It tells a story of perspicuous simplicity, yet of enthralling interest. It presents clearly defined characters in natural relations to each other. It is vitalized by a steady dramatic movement, that increases in force and speed till it reaches an electrical climax and a beautiful culmination. It is adequately freighted — without being burdened — with situations that excite the imagination and touch the heart. Its spirit is sympathetic with virtue and gentleness, and, therefore, it captivates the general instincts of human nature. Above all, it is imaginative: it idealizes reality, and does not weary by presenting character and experience in the garb of prosy fact. Viewed as an ideal fabric, it is a drama without serious defect. Its salient blemish is one of literary art: that is to say, there is some tinsel in its language — an infusion of the paste-diamond element that is peculiar to most of Bulwer's works. But, little faults dwindle to nothing alongside of great merits. "Richelieu" is a play that constantly affords pleasure, by procuring and extolling — under deeply interesting and highly picturesque conditions of circumstance — the victory of good over evil. To have written a drama which thus makes its spectators happier and better for their seeing of it, is to have deserved the gratitude of the world. Considerate judgment will not dwell with censure upon the slight defect of an occasional tawdry line in a drama so radically powerful and brilliant.

The character of Richelieu, as it is herein portrayed, is higher and finer — as it ought to be — than that of the historic Cardinal. Richelieu was not, in actual life, the noble spirit that he is in this rosy fiction. The dramatist has depicted him as just, wise, kind, gentle, tolerant of weakness, sympathetic with virtue and innocence, superior to trials, steadfast in danger, sensitive to every sweet and poetic influence, and

12

only hostile and bitter when confronted with tyranny and wrong. The lower side of his nature, to be sure, is craft: but it is the craft of a philosopher and not of a trickster. When Richelieu uses indirection, it is such indirection as a deep knowledge of human nature and of worldly affairs has taught him to be essential in the conduct of life and the government of mankind. He never resorts to the skin of the fox till the skin of the lion has proved too short. In this drama he is shown in the expenditure of great powers upon small affairs — in the protection of a pair of young lovers, and in the defeat of a political intrigue: but these affairs are representative of what, in fact, were the prominent occupations of his life, and of what, equally in fact, are the universal occupations of the human race. Love, fame, wealth, power — these are at once the sources and the objects of all human action; and these are the elements upon which the force of Richelieu is seen to be expended. He is presented as a man of potent intellect and pure sensibility; and, notwithstanding his little vanities and the pettiness of the designs amid which he moves, his nature never declines from a stately and imperial individualism. The charm of the character grows out of this relation of it to its circumstances. Richelieu is the embodiment of virtuous power, shown in its grandest phase and function as the protector of innocent weakness. Seeing this aged priest, as he rises in the eye of the imagination, the observer instinctively feels, without pausing to reflect upon it, that this is a grand and noble old man, in whom the affections live an immortal life, who will be as true as steel to all that is good and pure, who wears with authentic right the royal garb of power, and who must as inevitably conquer and dominate as the sun must rise.   W. W.

II.—FACTS IN THE LIFE OF RICHELIEU.

Armand Jean du Plessis, Cardinal, and Duc de Richelieu, was born, in Paris, in 1585. He was a member of a noble family, and in early youth was destined for the Army; but, upon his brother's resignation of the See of Luçon, he embraced an opportunity, then presented, to dedicate himself to the service of the Church. Having studied theology, at the college of Navarre, he was, in 1607, consecrated Bishop of Luçon. His earlier priestly endeavours were devoted to the conversion of the Huguenot Calvinists. In 1614 he was chosen Deputy to the State-General. His eloquence attracted notice, and he was presently named almoner to Marie de Medicis, widow of Henri IV. and mother to Louis XIII. A little later he became Secretary of State for foreign affairs and for war. He had enjoyed, for a time, at this period in his career, the protection of Marshal d'Ancre, the favourite of the queen; but, in the commotion which attended the ruin and murder of that minister,—who was assassinated in the Louvre, April 24th, 1617,—the star of his fortunes suffered a temporary eclipse. He was banished to Luçon, and afterwards to Avignon, where he devoted his talents to the writing of theological treatises. But he was presently fortunate enough to effect a formal reconciliation between Louis XIII. and the queen; and in 1622, at the age of 37, he was created Cardinal. Two years later he became Prime Minister of France. His government was characterized by great power and splendour, and by marvellous success. He waged a deadly war against the Huguenots, and utterly subdued them. His siege and capture of Rochelle, in 1628, was an incident of this war. In 1635 he founded the French Academy. The chief work of his life was the maintenance of French supremacy in the affairs of continental Europe, by resistance to the encroachments of the [Austrian] House of Hapsburg. He built the Palais Cardinal, now called the Palais Royal,—which is, in part, the scene of Bulwer's drama,—and he rebuilt and beautified the College of Sorbonne. Several conspiracies were formed against the Cardinal; but his force of character, his sagacity, and his tremendous energy of purpose and action thwarted and subdued them all. The day on which Richelieu discomfited one of the most formidable of these plots—in which the king was a participant —was called the Day of Dupes; from the fact that all the persons concerned in it were duped by the sagacious and expeditious Cardinal. Richelieu died on the 4th of December, 1642. He had named Cardinal Mazarin as his successor. The student is referred to three lives of this famous statesman: by Aubrey, 1660; by John Le Clerc, 1718; and by Joy, 1806.   W. W.

III.—THE AUTHOR'S PREFACE TO RICHELIEU.

The administration of Cardinal Richelieu—whom, despite all his darker qualities, Voltaire and history justly consider the true architect of the French monarchy, and the great parent of French civilization—is characterized by features alike tragic and comic. A weak king, an ambitious favourite; a despicable conspiracy against the Minister, nearly always associated with a dangerous treason against the State;—these, with little variety of names and dates, constitute the eventful cycle through which, with a dazzling ease and an arrogant confidence, the great luminary fulfilled its destinies. Blent together, in startling contrast, we see the grandest achievements and the pettiest agents — the spy — the mistress — the capuchin : — the destruction of feudalism — the humiliation of Austria — the dismemberment of Spain.

Richelieu himself is still what he was in his own day — a man of two characters. If, on the one hand, he is justly represented as inflexible and vindictive, crafty and unscrupulous; so, on the other, it cannot be denied that he was placed in times in which the long impunity of every license required stern examples; that he was beset by perils and intrigues which gave a certain excuse to the subtlest inventions of self-defense; that his ambition was inseparably connected with a passionate love for the glory of his country; and that, if he was her dictator, he was not less her benefactor. It has been fairly remarked, by the most impartial historians, that he was no less generous to merit than severe to crime; that, in the various departments of the State, the Army, and the Church, he selected and distinguished the ablest aspirants; that the wars which he conducted were, for the most part, essential to the preservation of France, and Europe itself, from the formidable encroachments of the Austrian House; that, in spite of those wars, the people were not oppressed with exorbitant imposts; and that he left the kingdom he had governed in a more flourishing and vigorous state than at any former period of the French history, or at the decease of Louis XIV.

The cabals formed against this great statesman were not carried on by the patriotism of public virtue nor the emulation of equal talent: they were but court struggles, in which the most worthless agents had recourse to the most desperate means. In each, as I have before observed, we see combined the twofold attempt to murder the minister and to betray the country. Such, then, are the agents, and such the designs with which truth, in the drama as in history, requires us to contrast the celebrated Cardinal; not disguising his foibles or his vices, but not unjust to the grander qualities — especially the love of country — by which they were often dignified, and, at times, redeemed.

The historical drama is the concentration of historical events. In the attempt to place upon the stage the picture of an era, that license with dates and details which poetry permits, and which the highest authorities in the drama of France herself have sanctioned, has been, though not unsparingly, indulged. The conspiracy of the Duc de Bouillon is, for instance, amalgamated with the *denouement* of the *Day of Dupes;* and circumstances connected with the treason of Cinq-Mars — whose brilliant youth and gloomy catastrophe tend to subvert poetic and historic justice, by seducing us to forget his base ingratitude and his perfidious apostacy — are identified with the fate of the earlier favourite, Baradas, whose sudden rise and as sudden fall passed into a proverb. I ought to add that the noble romance of " Cinq-Mars " suggested one of the scenes in the fifth act ; and that for the conception of some portion of the intrigue connected with De Mauprat and Julie, I am, with great alterations of incident, and considerable if not entire reconstruction of character, indebted to an early and admirable novel by the author of " Picciola."

London, March, 1839.   E. L. B.

IV.—HISTORICAL HINTS FOR RICHELIEU.

The Count de Soissons and the Duke de Bouillon had a good army, and they knew how to use it ; and, for the greater certainty, resolved that, whilst this army should advance, they would assassinate the Cardinal, and stir up Paris to revolt.   *   *   *   The conspirators made a treaty with Spain to introduce her troops into France, and to throw everything into confusion by a Regency, which they thought would follow, and by which each one hoped to profit.   *   +   *   Richelieu had lost all his favour, and retained only the advantage of being necessary.   His good fortune ordained, at the last, that the plot should be discovered, and that a copy of the treaty should fall into his hands.—VOLTAIRE.

V.—NOTES TO RICHELIEU.

1 Epistemon speaks of Cleopatra as a crier of onions in the other world. " Her kingdom produced exceeding good ones, in the opinion of the Israelites.   Besides, of the two pearls of inestimable price which that queen owned, she, having caused her lover Antony to swallow one, dissolved in vinegar, intended to regale him with the second, if she had not been hindered.   Perhaps it was by way of punishment for this prodigality that she is reduced to sell onions — that is, such fruit as the Latins call unions, a sort of onions—as well as pearls."—RABELAIS.

2 Daphne was loved and pursued by Apollo : when on the point of being overtaken by him she prayed for aid, and was instantly metamorphosed into a laurel tree.

3 Olivares, Minister of Spain.

4 In six months the King made Baradas " First Esquire," " First Gentleman of the Chamber," " Captain of St. Germain," and " Lieut. of the King in Champagne."   In still less time he was turned out of all, and the ruins of his grandeur left him hardly enough to pay his debts. His sudden rise and as sudden fall passed into a proverb, so that we say, to signify a great fortune dissipated as soon as acquired, in common parlance—" The fortune of Baradas."—ANQUETIL.

5 Richelieu did, in fact, so thoroughly associate himself with the State, that, in cases where the extreme penalty of the law had been incurred, Le Clerc justly observes, he was more inexorable to those he had favoured—even to his own connections—than to other and more indifferent offenders. As in Venice (where the favourite aphorism was, "Venice first, Christianity next") so with Richelieu; the primary consideration was, "what will be best for the country?" On his death-bed he was asked if he forgave his enemies. He replied, "I never had any but those of the State." And this was true enough, for Richelieu and the State were one.

6 There are many anecdotes of the irony, often so terrible, in which Richelieu indulged. But he had a love for humour in its more hearty and genial shape. He would send for Boisrobert "to make him laugh," and grave ministers and magnates waited in the ante-room while the great Cardinal listened and responded to the sallies of the lively wit.

7 The Abbé Arnaud tells us that the queen was a little avenged on the Cardinal by the ill-success of the tragic comedy of "Mirame"—more than suspected to be his own, though presented to the world under the foster name of Desmarets. Its representation (says Pelisson), cost him 300,000 crowns. He was so transported out of himself by the performance that at one time he thrust his person half out of his box to show himself to the assembly; at another time he imposed silence on the audience that they might not lose the still more beautiful passages. He said afterwards to Desmarets: "After all, the French will never have any taste—they were not pleased with Mirame!"

8 Vialart remarque une chose qui peut expliquer la conduite de Richelieu en d'autres circonstances: c'est que les seigneurs à qui leur naissance ou leur mérite pouvoit permettre des prétensions, il avoit pour système, de leur accorder au de la même de leurs droits et de leur esperances, mais, aussi une fois comblés—si, au lieu de reconnoitre ses services ils se levoient contre lui, il les traitot misericorde.—ANQUETIL. See also the "Political Testament," and the "Memoires de Cardinal Richelieu," in Petitot's collection.

9 "So much a fanatic, so much a knave, founder of the 'Religieuses' of Calvary, a maker of verses." Thus speaks Voltaire of Father Joseph. His talents and influence with Richelieu, grossly exaggerated in his own day, are now rightly estimated. He was, in fact, an indefatigable man; carrying with his enterprizes the activity, the suppleness, the stubbornness necessary to make them succeed.—ANQUETIL. He wrote a Latin poem called "La Turciade," in which he sought to excite the kingdoms of Christians against the Turks. But the inspiration of Tyrtæus was

denied to Father Joseph. His hair was red; but for fear of displeasing the King, who detested red hair, he used leaden combs, which gave it a dark color.

¹⁰ Richelieu was commonly supposed, though I cannot say I find much evidence for it, to have been too presuming in an interview with Anne of Austria (the Queen), and to have bitterly resented the contempt she expressed for him.

¹¹ Richelieu not only employed the lowest, but would often consult men commonly esteemed the dullest. "He said that, in matters of the greatest importance, he had found, by experiment, that the least wise often suggested the best expedients."—LE CLERC.

¹² Both Richelieu and Joseph were originally intended for the profession of arms. Joseph had served, before he obeyed the spiritual inspiration to become a Capuchin. The death of his brother opened to Richelieu the Bishopric of Luçon; but his military propensities were as strong as his priestly ambition. I need scarcely add that the Cardinal, during his brilliant campaign in Italy, marched at the head of his troops, in complete armour. It was under his administration that occurred the last example of proclaiming war by the chivalric defiance of herald and cartel.

¹³ Richelieu valued himself much on his personal activity; for his vanity was as universal as his ambition. A nobleman at the house of Grammont one day found him employed in *jumping*, and, with all the *savoir vivre* of a Frenchman and a courtier, offered to jump against him. He suffered the Cardinal to jump higher, and soon after found himself rewarded by an appointment. Yet, strangely enough, this vanity did not lead to a patronage injurious to the State; for never before in France was ability made so essential a requisite in promotion. He was lucky in finding the cleverest men among his adroitest flatterers.

¹⁴ Voltaire openly charges Richelieu with being the lover of Marion de Lorme. The great poet of France, Victor Hugo, has sacrificed History to adorn her with qualities which certainly were not added to her personal charms. She was not less perfidious than beautiful. Le Clerc properly refutes the accusation of Voltaire against the discretion of Richelieu; and says, very justly, that, if the great minister had the frailties of human nature, he learnt how to veil them,— at least when he obtained the scarlet. In earlier life he had been prone to gallantries which a little prepossessed the King (who was formal and decorous, and threw a singular coldness into the few attachments he permitted to himself) against the aspiring intriguer. But these graver occupations died away in the engagement of higher pursuits or of darker passions.

15 The guard attached to Richelieu's person was, in the first instance, fifty soldiers, afterward increased to two companies of cavalry and two hundred musketeers. Huguet is, therefore, to be considered merely as the lieutenant of a small detachment of this little army.

16 Joseph's ambition was not, however, so moderate; he refused a bishopric, and desired the Cardinal's hat, for which favour Richelieu openly supplicated the Holy See, but contrived, somehow or other, never to effect it, although two ambassadors applied for it at Rome.

17 The peculiar religion of Père Joseph may be illustrated by the following anecdote: An officer, whom he had dismissed upon an expedition into Germany, moved by conscience at the orders he had received, returned for further explanations, and found the Capuchin *disant sa masse.* He approached and whispered: " But, my father, if these people defend themselves——" " Kill all," (Qu'on tue tout,) answered the good father, continuing his devotion.

18 Voltaire has a striking passage on the singular fate of Richelieu, recalled every hour from his gigantic schemes to frustrate some miserable cabal of the ante-room. Richelieu would often exclaim that " Six pieds de terre (as he called the king's cabinet) lui donnaient plus de peine que tout le reste de l'Europe." The death of Wallenstein, sacrificed by the Emperor Ferdinand, produced a most lively impression upon Richelieu. He found many traits of comparison between Ferdinand and Louis— Wallenstein and himself. In the memoirs—now regarded by the best authorities as written by his sanction, and in great part by himself—the great Frenchman bursts (when alluding to Wallenstein's murder) into a touching and pathetic anathema on the *misere de cette vie* of dependence on jealous and timid royalty, which he himself, while he wrote, sustained. It is worthy of remark, that it was precisely at the period of Wallenstein's death that Richelieu obtained from the king an augmentation of his guard.

19 The fear and hatred which Richelieu generally inspired were not shared by his dependents and those about his person, who are said to have adored him. His servants looked upon him as the best of masters.—LE CLERC. In fact, although he was proud and choleric, he was at the same time no less affable and generous to those who served, than severe to those who opposed him.

20 In common with his contemporaries, Richelieu was credulous as to the divinations of astrology. He was too fortunate a man not to be superstitious.

21 Louis XIII. is said to have possessed some natural talents, and in earlier youth to have exhibited the germs of noble qualities; but a blight

seemed to have passed over his maturer life. Personally brave, but morally timid, always governed, whether by his mother or his minister, and always repining at the yoke,— the only affection amounting to a passion that he betrayed was for the sports of the field. Yet it was his crowning weakness (and this throws a kind of false interest over his character) to wish to be loved. He himself loved no one. He suffered the only woman who seems to have been attached to him to wither in a convent; he gave up favourite after favourite to exile or the block. When Richelieu died he said, coldly, "There is a great politician dead!" And when the ill-fated, but unprincipled Cinq-Mars, whom he called dear friend, was beheaded, he drew out his watch at the fatal hour, and said, with a smile: "I think at this moment the dear friend makes an ugly face." Nevertheless, his conscience at times (for he was devout and superstitious), made him gentle, and his pride and his honour would often, when least expected, rouse him into haughty but brief resistance to the despotism under which he lived.

22 One of Richelieu's severest and least politic laws was that which made duelling a capital crime. Never was the punishment against the offence more relentlessly enforced; and never were duels so desperate and so numerous. The punishment of death must be evidently ineffectual so long as to refuse a duel is to be dishonoured, and so long as men hold the doctrine, however wrong, that it is better to part with the life that Heaven gave than with the honour that man makes. In fact, the greater the danger he incurred, the greater was the punctilio of that cavalier of the time in braving it.

23 In his Memoirs Richelieu gives an amusing account of the insolence and arts of Baradas, and observes with indignant astonishment that the favourite was never weary of repeating to the king that he (Baradas) would have made just as great a minister as Richelieu. It is on the attachment of Baradas to La Cressias, a maid of honour to the Queen-Mother, of whom, according to Baradas, the King was enamoured also, that his love for the Julie de Mortemar of the play has been founded. The secret of Baradas' sudden and extraordinary influence with the King seems to rest in the personal adoration which he professed for Louis, with whom he affected all the jealousy of a lover, but whom he flattered with the ardent chivalry of a knight. Even after his disgrace he placed upon his banner, "Fiat voluntas tua."

24 Of the haughty and rebuking tone which Richelieu assumed in his expostulations with the King, Montesquieu says: "He degraded the King, but he made illustrious the reign." But however proud and choleric in his disputes with Louis, the Cardinal did not always disdain

recourse to the arts of the courtier. Once, after an angry discussion with the King, in which, as usual, Richelieu got the better, Louis, as they quitted the palace together, said, rudely, "Go first—you are *indeed* the King of France." "If I pass out first," replied the minister, after a moment's hesitation, and with great adroitness, "it is only as the humblest of your servants;" and he took a *flambeau* from one of the pages, to light the king as he walked before him.

25 According to the custom of Louis XIII., to cause the arrest of a person for a State crime, and to have him put to death, was very nearly the same thing.—LE CLERC.

26 Like Cromwell and Rienzi, Richelieu appears to have been easily moved to tears. The Queen-Mother, who put the hardest interpretation on that humane weakness which is natural with very excitable temperaments, said: "He weeps whenever he chooses." It is recorded of him that when his affairs did not succeed he was cast down and frightened, and when he had obtained that which he desired he was proud and insulting.

27 This alludes to Hildebrand (Gregory VII.), who carried his authority so far as to send legates into all the kingdoms of Europe to support his rights.

28 When Popilius Lenas was sent as ambassador to Antiochus, King of Syria, whom the Roman Senate wished to restrain from hostilities against Egypt, he gave the King the letter of the Senate, which he read; and promised to take into consideration. Then, as Antiochus was about marching upon Alexandria, Popilius described with his cane a circle, in the sand, round the king, and ordered him not to stir out of it until he had given a decisive answer, at the risk of Rome's displeasure. This boldness so frightened Antiochus that he at once yielded to the demand.

29 The passion of the drama requires this catastrophe for Baradas. He, however, survived his disgrace, though stripped of all his rapidly acquired fortunes; and the daring that belonged to his character won him distinction in foreign service. He returned to France after Richelieu's death, but never regained the same court influence. He had taken the vows of a Knight of Malta, and Louis made him a Prior.

30 The sudden resuscitation of Richelieu (not to strain too much on the real passion which supports him in this scene) is in conformance with the more dissimulating part of his character. The extraordinary mobility of his countenance (latterly so death-like, save when the mind spoke in the features), always lent itself to stage effect of this nature. The Queen-Mother said of him that she had seen him one moment so feeble,

cast-down and "semi-mort," that he seemed on the point of giving up the ghost; and the next moment he would start up, full of animation and energy.

_____

Ruelle, or Reuil, is a town of France, situated at the foot of Mont Valerien, about five miles from Paris.

Joseph, the Capuchin, was commonly called Father Joseph. He was a wily *intriguant*, and rendered much service to Richelieu. He died, of apoplexy, in 1638.

The author's dedication of "Richelieu," which, it may be assumed, he wished should accompany every edition of the play, is in the following words: "To the Marquis of Lansdowne, K. G., &c., &c., this drama is inscribed, in tribute to the talents which command, and the qualities which endear, respect."

The author of "Picciola" was Joseph Xavier Boniface Saintine. He was born at Paris, July 10th, 1798, and died there, January 21st, 1865. He published dramas, poems, and romances, a collection of philosophical stories, called "Jonathan, the Visionary," and a "History of the Wars in Italy." For "Picciola," his most popular work, he received the Monthyon Prize, in 1837. This novel passed through ten editions within eight years, and it has been translated into several languages.

The novel of "Cinq-Mars," which is mentioned in Bulwer's preface to "Richelieu" as, in part, the basis of the piece, was written by Alfred Victor, Count de Vigny, a native of France, born at Loche, in 1799. "Cinq-Mars" was published in 1826, and it has been translated into several languages. De Vigny won a bright distinction, both as a poet and a novelist. He wrote several plays, one of which illustrates the gloomy fate of Chatterton. De Vigny was a member of the French Academy. He died in 1863.

Henry Coiffier de Ruzè, Marquis de Cinq-Mars, was born in France, in 1620. At the age of 18 he was presented at the court of Louis XIII., by Cardinal Richelieu, and thereafter he soon became a favourite to the king. Ambition, commingled with hatred of Richelieu, presently led him to form a conspiracy against the Cardinal, in which the king himself, and his brother Gaston, Duc d'Orleans, participated. The plot miscarried: the Cardinal prevailed: and Cinq-Mars was beheaded, together with his friend the Councillor de Thou, at Lyons, September 12th, 1642.

Tyrtæus, mentioned above, was a Greek poet of the 7th century, B. C. He was a deformed man, blind of one eye, and was a school-master. The Spartans, being at war with the Messenians, obeying an oracle, asked the Athenians for a leader. The Athenians sent to them Tyrtæus, as the most unfit captain that could be chosen; but Tyrtæus so inspired the Spartans by his war-songs that they were victorious, and subdued their foes. The fragments of the poems of Tyrtæus are in Gaisford's "Poetæ Minores Greci," translated into English verse by Polwhele, 1786-'92.

The Capuchins were a body of friars, of the order of St. Francis, instituted by Matteo Baschi, in 1525, and established under Pope Clement VII., in 1529. They were at first called Friars Hermits Minor. Their order was confirmed, in 1536, by Pope Paul III., who named them Capuchins of the Order of Friars Minor. Their name was derived from the Latin designation [*Caputium*] of the cowl that they wore. This head-gear was shaped like a sugar-loaf. The Capuchins were introduced into France in 1573-'74.

Marie de Medicis, the Queen-mother, was born at Florence, in 1573; made mischief for everybody, all her days; was exiled by Richelieu; and died, at Cologne, in destitution, in 1642. Louis XIII., her son, was born at Fontainebleu, September 27th, 1601; came to the throne of France in 1610; and died at St. Germaine, May 14th, 1643.

Many of the foregoing notes are by the author. Several of them have been shortened and otherwise altered, and many new ones have been introduced. There are, in the original, other notes, which relate to passages not included in this version of the drama.—W. W.

www.ingramcontent.com/pod-product-compliance
Lightning Source LLC
Chambersburg PA
CBHW031109020726
47495CB00007B/2119